WINNER OF THE CRIME WRITERS' ASSOCIATION
DEBUT DAGGER

WINNER OF THE 2018 INDIE DEBUT FICTION AWARD

SHORTLISTED FOR LITERARY FICTION BOOK OF
THE YEAR, ABIA AWARDS 2018

SHORTLISTED FOR THE MATT RICHELL AWARD FOR
NEW WRITER OF THE YEAR, ABIA AWARDS 2018

SHORTLISTED FOR THE NED KELLY AWARD FOR
BEST FIRST FICTION 2018

'This book is SO good. Published to huge acclaim in Australia, *Into the River* is dark, unsettling and makes for compulsive reading'

Hannah Richell, author of *Secrets of the Tides*

'Brimming with tension and menace… an unforgettable story extremely well told. It had my heart racing and breaking in equal measure'

Sarah Bailey, author of *The Dark Lake*

'Part crime fiction, part coming of age tale – a masterful evocation of a childhood gone awry'

Chris Hammer, author of *Scrublands*

'I had a passionate response to this book; uncrowded, clean, powerful story-telling that held me in its grip… Writing like this is precious and rare'

Sofie Laguna, author of *The Eye of the Sheep*

Into
the
River

MARK BRANDI

Legend Press Ltd, 107-111 Fleet Street, London, EC4A 2AB
info@legend-paperbooks.co.uk | www.legendpress.co.uk

Contents © Mark Brandi 2019
First published by Hachette Australia (an imprint of Hachette Australia Pty
Limited), Level 17, 207 Kent Street, Sydney NSW 2000
www.hachette.com.au

Print ISBN 978-1-78955-012-2
Ebook ISBN 978-1-78955-011-5
Set in Times. Printing managed by Jellyfish Solutions Ltd.
Cover design by Steve Marking | www.stevemarking.com

After initially studying law, then completing a degree in criminal justice, **Mark Brandi** worked extensively in corrections and emergency services before turning his hand to writing. His shorter pieces appear in *The Guardian*, *The Age*, *The Big Issue*, and in journals both in Australia and overseas. His writing is sometimes heard on Australia's ABC Radio National.

Originally from Italy, growing up in a rural Australian town (in a pub) continues to influence his creative focus. He now lives in Melbourne. His second novel, *The Rip*, will be published by Legend Press in 2020.

Follow Mark at
www.markbrandi.com
or on Twitter
@mb_randi

For Tomassina and Tommaso

Prologue

Dad told them never to cross the highway.

But the dam hadn't been much good that day. It was a green dam and Jed told Danny there were no yabbies in green dams, only fish if you're lucky. Yabbies were only in muddy dams. But Danny, as usual, reckoned he knew better.

They caught nothing, so Jed got bored and reckoned they should go to the river, just for a look. But they had to cross the highway to get there.

'What if Dad finds out?' Danny said.

Jed shrugged. 'How would he?'

They left the nets at the dam and Jed pushed down the lower lines of the fence with his foot so Danny could climb through without getting scratched by the barbed wire.

A long truck, belting north toward town, howled its horn as it tore past, destined for the abattoir. The smell of sheep shit and oily wool lingered, as Jed and Danny slid down the steep, stony embankment to the edge of the highway.

Jed was a good foot taller than Danny and could see down the road until it curved away to the west. To the east of the curve was a flat, yellow patchwork of paddocks that disappeared in a shimmer below the stony face of the Grampians, looming like a tidal wave at the horizon.

Above the range, blue-black clouds billowed and ruptured, and a grey veil descended across the mountains. The wind shifted quickly from the southwest to a cooler southerly, and Jed could tell the weather was coming soon. He could smell it, like the start of rain falling on a hot road. Like wet cement.

Then, without warning, Danny took off across the highway. Jed called out for him to stop, but his voice was lost in the wind as Danny disappeared down the slope on the other side.

The river. *Shit*. Danny couldn't swim.

Jed heard the nearing rumble of another truck, so he ran while he had the chance. The wind blew at him, willing him back. But he was a good runner and he pushed against it, the highway smooth and warm under his bare feet. He made it to the dry grassy edge, eyes watering and chest heaving. The truck's horn blasted as it passed.

He couldn't see Danny anywhere.

'Danny!' he yelled. Across a lazy field of long yellow weeds, a tall row of eucalypts swayed as the air whooshed through their branches. Just past those trees, he knew the river ran deep and strong.

'Danny!' The wind ripped his calls away and he could hear the coming thunder of another truck headed west.

Jed ran through the weeds and toward the trees, his legs bouncing on the dumb earth like rubber. He imagined telling his mum, trying to explain, but she'd never believe him. For certain, his dad would beat the living shit out of him, probably break some bones – maybe even kill him.

He would have to run away, go live in the bush somewhere, or the city.

He could never go back home.

'Danny!' he screamed. Startled, a cluster of sulphur-crested cockatoos erupted from the high branches of the eucalypts, squawking and screeching, their pure white feathers stark against the blackening sky.

The truck roared past behind him and, in the quiet after,

Jed could hear the river surge, hidden deep within the trees and scrub.

* * *

As he first caught sight of water, flowing fast beyond a row of trees and thick shrubbery, the wind suddenly relented. He called out again, his voice broken and throat raw. Then, near the river, from behind a prickle bush, his brother stepped into view, with eyes wide and cheeks flushed red.

Jed felt a march of hot anger rise in his chest.

'You'll pay for that,' he said. 'You wait til later.'

Danny smiled. 'But I found something. Quick, come look!'

Jed followed him down to the river's edge, to where an ancient ghost gum had fallen into purpose, forming a long bridge across the water, its thick roots upended by rain, the river and time.

'There!' Danny pointed.

'Big deal,' Jed shrugged. 'A tree fell down.' He looked up at the sky closing in – for certain, they'd be riding home wet and cold. Danny screwed up his face and pointed again.

'Nah, look properly! Under the tree. It's stuck.'

Jed looked at the dead tree, the black rush beneath and the gathering yellow foam until he saw what Danny was pointing at – a green wheelie bin, wedged under the middle of the trunk, with water streaming along its sides.

'It's a rubbish bin,' Jed said. 'So what?'

Danny's face dropped. But Jed was intrigued. What was a town bin doing way out here?

He moved closer to the river, stepping through the low branches and over rocks to the soft earth at the water's edge. He took hold of a root, a long dead artery, and leaned over the river, as close as he could without getting wet.

Rain began to fall through the canopy of eucalypts, but Jed wasn't thinking about that now. He climbed aboard the slippery trunk and moved closer, gripping a slick flex of branches as he stepped slowly across the bridge.

Danny watched from the riverbank. 'Be careful,' he said. But the rain was falling heavily and Jed couldn't hear a word.

As he got closer to the middle of the river, Jed thought he could see bolts screwed into the top of the bin. There were a lot of them, all around the edge of the lid.

It looked like someone wanted it closed up really tight. Like they didn't want it ever to be opened.

Like they didn't want what was in there to ever come out.

Part One

One

B en saw the ambulance up the street when he was coming
home from footy training, but he didn't think that much
of it. When he got inside, his mum and dad were quiet, looking
at the telly. *The Wonder Years* was on, but the sound was
turned off. Then the phone rang and his mum ran to it, almost
like she knew it was coming.

* * *

At dinnertime, his dad put on the black-and-white telly in the
kitchen. *The A-Team* was on and Hannibal and Murdock were
making some sort of catapult to help them escape from prison.
They were using a bed frame, steel springs and even the bed
sheets to make it. They had tools though, which really didn't
make sense if they were supposed to be in prison.

   Mum and Dad were both still quiet and Ben tried to think
of something to say, so he told them about the ambulance up
the road. Dad stopped chewing, looked at Mum and said, 'Ah
yeah.' Then he went back to his chops and *The A-Team*. Mum
didn't say anything.

* * *

After dinner, Mum served dessert, which was weird because they only ever had dessert on Sundays if they sat in the special room. In the special room they would sometimes have chocolate mousse with chopped-up nuts on top, especially if guests came over. Even with chocolate mousse, Ben didn't like the special room because it didn't have a telly in it, and the chairs were uncomfortable.

This time though, they were in the kitchen and there was no chocolate mousse. It was just Neapolitan ice-cream, but only the vanilla and strawberry were left. Ben never understood why his mum didn't just buy chocolate, but he never asked about it.

Dad went back to the couch and turned on the big telly, but Mum sat there at the kitchen table and watched Ben eat the ice-cream until he was finished. Then, after he'd licked all the melted bits at the bottom of the bowl, she told him that Daisy was dead. She had hanged herself on the clothesline.

No one said anything else after that.

* * *

Daisy Wolfe was fourteen, three years older than Ben, and they got on the same bus at the same stop. She never talked to anyone much, just chewed gum and listened to her Walkman.

One time, this total psycho grade six kid, Tom Joiner, was gonna bash Ben behind the bus shelter for no reason at all. But Daisy found out, grabbed hold of him and choked him in a headlock til he cried. She was pretty tough for a girl. And Ben kind of loved her a bit after that, though never told anyone.

He wondered why she'd done it, why she hanged herself. Maybe she was failing at high school or something. Or maybe the kids were teasing her. He didn't reckon it would be that, but. She was pretty good looking. 'Very popular with the boys' – that's what his mum said.

She must have been upset about something though. Ben wondered why she didn't just run away. That's what he would do if things ever got really bad. He'd never hang himself, no way. And definitely not in the backyard where his mum would find him.

He tried to imagine Daisy's body hanging from that old steel clothesline, creaking as it shifted in the wind. He could see her dark eyes and her legs, perfectly white, swinging in the air.

Then the wind would blow harder, the clothesline would creak, and her summer school dress ripple as the shit and piss slid down those smooth, creamy legs. He knew about the shit and piss because Fab had told him that's what happens. And Fab's cousin, Marco, had told him about it. Marco was eighteen and from Melbourne, and he knew about things like that, so Fab said it must be true.

Ben imagined that's how Daisy's younger brother, Joe, would have found her, with the shit and piss running down her legs. Just before she did it, she'd given Joe fifty cents to buy mixed lollies from the milk bar. He'd bought raspberry jubes, jelly teeth and a 'Big Boss' cigar. The milk bar was opposite the footy oval and Ben had seen him walking past, showing off with his cigar. Joe didn't know then that Ben and Fab had smashed his cubbyhouse at the block over the back. And he didn't know the real reason Daisy had given him fifty cents.

Ben heard his mum say that Joe had tried to wake Daisy up. That he got hold of her legs, tried to lift her, and was screaming at her to stop mucking around and just wake up. That's how Mrs Pickering, who lived next door, found out – she heard Joe crying like she'd never heard before. She called the ambulance and all that, but it was way too late.

And Mum said that Joe would never recover. But Ben didn't really know what she meant by that.

* * *

They buried Daisy quick. That's what Ben's dad said, that it was really quick. Mum said, quietly, they were doing it quick because of what she did. Ben wondered if that was because she'd start rotting sooner than normal, but he thought he better not ask.

The funeral was just a couple of days later, a Saturday. It was the only time Ben had ever seen his dad in a suit. It was navy blue and it made him look like the prime minister, but smaller and with brown hair. Mum even made him put a tie on. She said it was the first time he'd worn one since their wedding day, but he hadn't needed to tie that one up. So Mum had to help him do it and it took ages.

After she got Dad sorted, she cooked pancakes, then got all dressed up in a black skirt and jacket. She even had lipstick on, which made her look a bit fancy. But no one hardly said a word.

Ben was happy though. Mainly because he was allowed to stay home on his own, eat pancakes, and watch cartoons.

* * *

Two days after the funeral, Ben's dad offered to get rid of the clothesline and Daisy's parents agreed. He put his long blue overalls on and got the angle grinder from the shed. Ben wanted to go with him, but Mum said no. She said it wouldn't be right. Then his dad said he could come to the tip after, which was even better. They always picked up some good stuff at the tip, and Ben liked chucking rocks at the feral cats.

Dad said he'd be about an hour, but he came back from the Wolfes' nearly right away, his face all white. Mum asked what had happened and Dad said that Mrs Wolfe told him to *get the fuck away from it you cunt* in a voice like he'd never heard from a woman.

So the clothesline stayed. They didn't go to the tip. And the Wolfes left town.

* * *

It was three months later that the new neighbour moved in.

'A Statesman De Ville,' his dad said, without shifting his gaze from the telly. It was Friday, so he was drinking a big bottle of beer without a glass. 'Nice car. Must be on good money.' Mum didn't say much about it, but slipped a cork coaster on the table, while his dad took a swig. The cork ones were for family – she had fancy wooden ones with pictures of kangaroos that she used for guests in the special room.

The news was on – it was something about the World Expo that had been on in Queensland and how they reckoned it was the best ever. Ben pretended to watch, but it was boring and he was mainly thinking about the new neighbour.

Ben wondered if the neighbour knew about the clothesline and the last thing that hung there. The clothesline that rattled in the wind when he rode his bike past, like it was calling him closer. The clothesline with its cold steel poles, bolts and wires, spinning forever in that relentless southerly wind.

In the front yard, weeds had sprouted and the grass had grown long. And that nice, shiny blue car just sat there in the driveway.

Two

Ben's family never went on holidays. His parents just weren't the type. The only one they'd been on was to Adelaide when he was four. The drive was really long to get there; he remembered that bit. Mum wanted to stop at a motel in some place called Kaniva, but Dad said he wanted to keep going because he was making good time. Ben remembered the drive, but he didn't remember much about Adelaide. The only thing he remembered was that his dad made him go into the sea.

He stood there, waist deep and with his back to the ocean, waving to his mum in her stripy green bikini. She was trying to take a photo, but was having trouble with the camera. Dad was trying to unscrew the flashcube, but it wouldn't come off. While Ben was watching all this, a wave smashed into him from behind. It flipped him upside down, the salty water filling his throat and lungs. He remembered his dad lifting him up out of the water, laughing, and carrying him back to the beach.

After that, Ben decided it was better to stay at home in the summer holidays.

At home, the days and weeks seemed to stretch on without end. He could daydream for hours, building imaginary worlds at the back of the yard, up near the shed. Whole civilisations rose and fell in the black soil of the vegie garden. Epic wars were won and lost.

He had all day to play with his dog, Sunny. Then, at night, he could lie in his bed til late, close his eyes and imagine colours and shapes and worlds more vivid than in any book he ever saw.

And he had yabbying. He loved yabbying and he couldn't go if they went on holidays. He'd always ask Fab to come because it wasn't as good on your own. If Fab couldn't come, he'd ask Shane, but Shane was a sook and always wanted to go home early. They were only really friends with Shane because his house had an in-ground pool and his mum cooked steak sandwiches for lunch. His dad had a red Porsche too, but you were never allowed inside it, or even close to it.

If he was desperate he might ask Johnno, but everyone knew that Johnno was a first-class dick.

He rang Fab first.

'Whatcha doin?'

'Nuthin. You?'

'Nuthin. What about tomorrow?'

'Dunno. You?'

'Dunno. Gonna be hot, but.'

'Yeah.'

'Wanna go yabbying?'

'Yeah, all right.'

'Near the Leviathan. S'posed to be a good spot.'

The only thing Ben and Fab ever disagreed on was bait. Ben preferred lamb's liver, left in the sun for a bit so it would get stinky. He reckoned yabbies could smell it. Fab reckoned yabbies couldn't smell anything underwater. He reckoned they preferred dog food because it had guts and organs and stuff in it. Pal dog food. He'd steal his mum's pantyhose and put chunks of Pal inside, then tie them to the bottom of the nets. The Pal was no good for handlines, but. It was way too soft.

Ben liked that Fab used different bait. He liked it because it meant he'd usually get more yabbies than Fab – it was one of the few things he was better at. He also liked it because it meant Fab brought the pantyhose. The soft, silky fabric and that dark patch in the middle part made him a bit horny. Fab's mum looked a bit like Ita Buttrose, but with darker hair.

Ben liked Ita Buttrose, even though she was a bit older. There was a photo of her in an old *Women's Weekly* he liked to look at sometimes. Fab reckoned that Wilbur Wilde was Ita Buttrose's boyfriend, that Marco had told him, but Ben reckoned that was bullshit. Wilbur Wilde played the saxophone on *Hey Hey It's Saturday* and wore sunglasses, even at night. He was pretty ugly.

Once, Ben stole a pair of pantyhose from Fab, took them home and hid them under his bed. He'd get them out at night sometimes, rub them against his bare thighs and imagine what they would feel like with a girl wearing them, a girl in his bed. Maybe Ita Buttrose. Or even Fab's mum.

It was a thought he nervously explored, his breath hot and fast, as he lifted the sheets and wanked as quietly as he could.

But he'd promised himself he'd stop doing that soon. Maybe once they started grade six.

* * *

They rode their bikes to the dam. Fab's bike had a buckled front wheel that rubbed against the brake pads, so it took ages. It was a pretty shit ride because it was hot and there were a lot of hills on the way there. It meant they couldn't take all the nets, so Fab was already pissed off that he'd have to use handlines. Plus, his buckled wheel was squeaking like crazy.

They'd have to walk home too, because they couldn't carry the yabbies on their bikes. Ben liked to use a bucket for his, with some water to keep them going til he got home. They would sometimes fight in the bucket and once you got them home, you'd find loose claws at the bottom that had been cleaved right off.

Ben's mum usually boiled the yabbies in a big pot. Ben

thought he could hear them scream as she dropped them in, but Fab reckoned it was just the gas inside their shells.

Fab used a wet hessian sack to carry his haul. Ben thought this was crazy because it was much harder to get them out, their claws would catch in the weave and, once loose, they'd snap angrily at your fingers. Fab agreed with Ben, but he said his dad told him to do it that way. And you didn't argue with Fab's dad.

Fab's dad worked at the timber mill. He did shift work, which means you sleep during the day and work at night. He once told Ben that he would take a shortcut through the cemetery if it was a full moon, to get home quicker. Ben couldn't imagine anything scarier than the cemetery at night. Except maybe for seeing Fab's dad in there.

Sometimes they got a lift home from yabbying if Fab's mum had the Pacer.

This was always better, because walking home when it was nearly dark was pretty scary. Not because they were worried about anything stupid like vampires, werewolves or stuff like that, but because of Jimmy Shine.

Jimmy Shine always seemed to somehow know where they were. He would drive up in his old cream ute and slow right down beside them. Jimmy Shine had a rotten face and wide straw hat. Jimmy Shine had bib-overalls and old-fashioned white cotton shirts with no collar. He was weird. They scared each other just talking about him. And the sight of any ute was enough to make them freeze. But lately, other things had been scaring Ben too.

Ben unpacked his gear on the dam bank. 'Are you gonna use the handlines?' he said. The dam was small with steep banks, which probably meant it was deep. And there wasn't much shade, just one stunted old gum tree near the fence, its leaves already drooping in the morning sun.

'Nah, just the nets first.'

Ben could tell from the look on Fab's face that he was pissed off about having only two nets, not to mention the long ride with a buckled wheel.

'What do ya reckon?' Ben said. 'Many yabbies?'

'Maybe.' Fab said. 'Could be poisoned, but.' He nodded to the round concrete vats buried deep within the soil beside the dam. You could only see the top of them, just a couple of feet of thick concrete poking up through the dirt. Fab reckoned they had something to do with the goldmine.

Fab pulled the pantyhose from his pocket and Ben felt a tingle in the tip of his dick. He turned away from Fab and focused on the sweaty liver, where flies were already gathering. The ants had noticed it too, marching fast in orderly lines from their holes. He looked down at his shorts and his dick bulged sideways, like someone had stuffed a banana down there. Not a big banana though, just one of those ladyfinger ones.

Ladyfingers. Ladies with soft fingers. Soft fingers for touching dicks.

He took a deep breath and started cutting the lengths of string for his handlines. 'Had a nightmare last night,' he said.

Fab cut a section of pantyhose and tied a knot in one end. 'Yeah, what happened?'

'Can't remember it all.' Ben scratched his head and looked down at his shorts. It had gone smaller, but was still visible. 'Had Daisy in it. She was in my room.' He pushed his dick down straight and turned back around.

Fab's eyes lit up. He put down his knife. 'No shit? What did she look like? Was she rotten or anything?'

'Nah, just really white. I was trying to get away from her.'

'Probably her ghost,' Fab said. He smiled at Ben. 'Are you sure it was a dream?'

'Piss off, will ya?' Ben checked the lengths of his lines. 'It's a bit creepy though. After what she did and all that.'

Fab returned to his bait, eyes downcast. He took a can-opener out of his hessian sack. 'Yeah, feel sorry for Joe.'

Ben still felt guilty about the cubbyhouse. He reckoned Fab did too.

'Why do you reckon she did it?' he said.

Fab shrugged as he worked around the lid of a can. 'Dunno.

I heard Johnno saying she was giving gobbies to some of the year twelve boys.'

'Gobbies?'

Fab scooped some dog food into the pantyhose with his fingers. 'A gobbie. A gob job.'

'A what?' Ben got a whiff of the dog food. It was rank.

'That's what they call it in Melbourne. Marco told me. Same as a head job. Like when a girl sucks on your dick. Or licks it.'

'Bullshit.'

'Nah, it is,' Fab said.

'Nah, I mean Johnno is full of shit. Daisy wouldn't do that.'

Fab shook his head. 'Johnno reckons his brother was getting them regular after school. Reckons they're all disappointed she's dead. That she was really good at it.'

'It's bullshit. No way would she have done that.'

Ben watched the ants gather at the edge of the liver, unsure about their next move. It was too big for them to carry and they seemed confused, breaking their orderly lines and walking into one another. He was trying very hard not to think about Daisy sucking his dick. Or licking it. Or what the difference was between the two.

'They've moved town now,' he said.

'Who?' Fab stood up, holding the net in his hands.

'The Wolfes.'

'Yeah, heard me mum say.' Fab widened his stance, ready to cast.

'Someone else living there now. Some bloke. Got a nice car.' Ben remembered what his dad had said. He liked talking about cars, especially to Fab who seemed to know about that sort of stuff. It made him feel like less of a kid. 'A Statesman De Ville. Blue. Really nice.' He didn't actually know what a Statesman De Ville was, so he hoped like anything that Fab wouldn't ask.

With the string line of the net in his left hand, Fab flung it like a frisbee with his right. It splashed just a few metres out and sunk fast into the muddy water. The black plastic float popped to the surface and Fab tied the string to a stick, before poking it into the dam bank. 'Ah well,' he said, rubbing his hands, 'maybe her ghost will be on to him then. Once she's done with you, of course.' He laughed. 'Might even give you a gobbie.'

'Rack off!'

Fab picked up another net. 'A ghost gobbie. That's pretty special. She'd like your stiffy for sure.' He pointed at Ben's shorts and laughed.

'Get stuffed, will ya!' Ben turned back around and checked. 'It's gone anyway.'

Ben still wondered why Daisy had hanged herself, but he didn't think it had anything to do with Johnno's story about head jobs. Either way, he didn't want to think about her for a while. Not if it meant more bad dreams.

He picked up the slimy liver just as a few ants climbed on board. The remaining army continued to trace the perimeter of where it had been, in blind disbelief.

He looked up to the sky where the sun was getting higher and hotter. They had a long day ahead and plenty of time. But he'd try to get Fab to finish a bit early, so maybe they could walk home in the daylight.

Three

Fab reckoned Ben's new neighbour was a secret agent. He said the blue car was like the James Bond one and it might change into a boat or something. He reckoned they should try to follow him, to see what he was up to.

Fab knew a fair bit about spies and secret agents because he'd seen a lot of videos about it, he reckoned. And he had this book called *Spycatcher* that he nicked from the newsagent. It had a cool black cover and he kept it in his desk at school. He said that he'd read it, but Ben didn't believe him. It was really thick and Fab wasn't even that good at reading. He wasn't that good at school in general, really. When Ben asked him what the book was about, he'd just say that it was top secret.

They kept an eye on the house for a couple of days, riding their bikes or walking past casually, or sometimes watching from behind the cars parked across the road. Nothing seemed to happen and they both got bored. On the third day, they snuck up the driveway to get a closer look at the car – it was clean and shiny, all chrome and blue steel. But they couldn't see inside because it had dark windows.

'Tinted,' Fab whispered. He nodded at Ben like this confirmed his theory. Then there was a heavy clunk inside the house. They stared at each other with wide eyes before running back down the driveway as fast as they could.

After, Fab called Ben a wuss for running, even though Ben thought Fab ran first. But he didn't say anything.

The car never seemed to go anywhere and the curtains of the house were always shut. Fab reckoned the neighbour was probably doing interrogations inside. He said there was stuff about that in the book, that they'd usually do it in the dark with a bright lamp shining in your eyes. Fab nicked his dad's binoculars and they climbed the plum tree in Ben's backyard to try to see in through the back, but Ben's dad caught them.

'He's on to us for sure,' Fab said.

'My dad?'

'Nah, the spy. Maybe we should back off a little. Get out of town. Let him think no one is watching.' Ben thought he could hear the edge of an American accent in Fab's voice, like he was pretending to be Harrison Ford or something. 'Maybe we should go camping.'

Ben was happy to go camping. They hadn't been in ages and the holidays were almost over. It'd be good to do something before they went back to school. But he didn't really care that much about the neighbour anymore.

* * *

Ben invited Johnno camping because he reckoned just the two of them alone was too weird. Ben knew Fab didn't like Johnno, no one really did, but he couldn't think of anyone else to ask apart from Shane, and he knew Shane got too homesick.

They camped where Fab's old house used to be, which was on a block of land near the Black Ranges, about five kilometres out of town. It was a good spot. The house had burnt down from an electrical fault, but Ben's dad said it was an insurance job. Ben didn't know what that meant. And when he asked, he still didn't get it. It just didn't make any sense that anyone would burn down their own house deliberately.

All that was left of the house was the concrete floor where the veranda used to be. It made a great cricket pitch. There was a large, steel hay shed still standing out the back where they could sleep, and a dam a bit further back for yabbying.

It wasn't til his mum had driven off up the highway that Fab showed Ben and Johnno what he'd brought. Hidden in the bottom of his backpack were four cans of Victoria Bitter that he'd nicked from his dad's beer fridge.

* * *

They didn't end up doing much yabbying on the first day. They played cricket the whole time. Ben had brought electrical tape and he wound it over one side of the ball, which made it swing through the air like crazy and sting like anything. Johnno cracked the shits after he kept getting out, so Fab and Ben kept playing without him.

Ben had a better batting technique than Fab, honed and refined in his backyard as he watched his reflection in the lounge room window. He modelled himself on Dean Jones, fast footwork and nimble. Quick singles.

Fab made up for his lack of style with a sharp eye and uncanny strength. He was wiry like a rabbit – and though his arms were skinny, and he was smaller than most, he bowled fast and hit hard. A bit of a slogger. And he always wanted to win, no matter what.

Though Ben hated to admit it, Fab was better at most physical things, like cricket or climbing or running, even though he never really looked the part. Fab never learned how to do things properly and he hardly ever went to training, but just picked things up really quickly. Ben couldn't quite match him, even though he was bigger and stronger. It annoyed him a bit.

In cricket, at least, Ben was a better fielder. He could hit the stumps from pretty much anywhere. The best arm in the district, his coach reckoned.

* * *

They played until the sun started to sink behind the ranges and it was too hard to see. That's when the wind picked up and the air turned cold. It got dark fast, so Fab yelled out to Johnno, who was sooking in the hay shed, to light the fire so they could cook some dinner.

They hadn't caught any yabbies, so it was just baked beans on burnt toast. Ben forgot to bring the toaster thing for the fire, so they did them on sticks and they went all black and tasted like shit. Fab ate quickly. He was keen to start on the cans of beer, still hidden in the bottom of his backpack.

'Maybe I should put them in the dam, to cool them down.' He mopped up the sweet, baked bean sauce with his fingers.

'I'm not havin any,' Johnno said, between mouthfuls of beans.

'You're such a sook.' Fab shook his head. 'Just eat your beans and keep quiet.'

Ben wasn't that keen on the booze either. He'd once had a sip of his dad's beer and it tasted sour. He'd hoped it would be like ginger beer, but it wasn't sweet at all and his dad had laughed at the face he pulled.

Still, Ben tried his best to sound excited. 'Don't worry about cooling them down, they'll be right.'

Fab put his plate down and went to his bag. Johnno poked Ben in the arm.

'Did ya hear about Daisy?' he said.

'About what?'

'About the head jobs? That she was mad for dick?' Johnno grinned. 'Did she ever suck on yours?'

'Piss off. It's bullshit anyway.'

'Nah, it's definitely not. My brother told me.'

'Your brother's full of shit too, then.'

Fab returned to the fire with two cans and glared at Johnno. 'Why dontcha go to bed,' he said.

Johnno stood up. 'I was goin anyway. Where's ya spare sleeping bag?'

'Near the back of the shed. Bring your own next time. And don't wank in my one.'

Fab passed Ben a can. They cracked the tops and knocked the cans together, like they'd seen on telly. They decided to both take a sip at the same time.

'One... two... three.' Fab slitted his eyes, but Ben could tell he was watching him, like he was making sure he had a drink. Like he knew.

'It's good, isn't it?' Fab said, licking his lips.

Ben wondered if he'd be able to tip out some of the can without Fab seeing.

'I really like it,' he said.

* * *

Ben and Fab stayed up by the fire, sipping slowly at their cans. It seemed like Fab definitely knew what Ben was planning and he watched him like a hawk.

The air had gotten colder and Johnno was snoring, lying up on two hay bales he'd pushed together like a mattress. As the wind swept the heat of the fire away, Fab fetched his sleeping bag. Ben seized the moment and tipped some of his can out. Fab unrolled the sleeping bag, sat back down and covered both their legs.

'Thanks.' Ben pulled the sleeping bag up to his waist. It was thin and rough. 'Jeez, it's an old sleeping bag,' he said.

Fab took a swig of his can. 'It's my father's. He's got mine.' He looked up at Johnno, on his hay-bale bed. 'Why did ya invite him for anyway?'

'He's not that bad.' Ben had a small sip.

'He's a dickhead and you know it. And he calls me a wog.'

Johnno did call him that. But only once. Still, Fab never forgot stuff like that.

It was after school when they were playing basketball, just a muckaround game. Johnno thought he was pretty tough, with his new crew cut and earring, and he called Fab a greasy wog for no reason at all. So Fab punched him in the guts and Johnno ran home to his mum.

Ben pushed a stick into the fire. 'Why do ya get so angry about it?'

'About what?'

'Being called a... you know.'

Fab took another drink. 'I dunno. Just don't like it. The way they say it.'

'Who, Pokey and that?'

'Yeah.'

It was mostly Pokey Stark who called Fab a wog. Pokey was a real shit. He had a rat's tail with bright blond tips and was always giving Fab grief. Other kids called him a wog behind his back, even some of his friends, but Fab didn't know about that and Ben definitely couldn't tell him. He'd be really upset if he found out.

'You're not really a wog though. I mean... you're normal.' Ben wasn't sure what else to say about it.

'Yeah. Well, I don't like it. And my father says I gotta stick up for myself.'

Ben picked up another stick and poked at the hot coals. 'Why do ya call him *father*? Why not dad?'

'Dunno.' Fab shifted closer to the flames. 'Just how it's always been.'

'How come your mum isn't *mother*, then?'

Fab shrugged. 'How should I know?'

'Does your father ever take you camping?'

Ben had imagined, more than once, that Fab's dad would go off into the forest somewhere alone, hunting animals with his bare hands, a huge hunting knife in his teeth. He was tall, big shouldered, and moved like he was strong. If he was honest, Ben was a bit scared of him, but he'd never tell Fab that.

'He doesn't take me. He sometimes goes with Sid.'

'Who's Sid?'

'This old man from the timber mill. Don't like him much. He stinks. They go somewhere in the Grampians.'

The beer was making Ben feel woozy. 'Do you reckon girls go too?'

'With him and Sid?'

'Nah, just generally. Do you reckon they go camping?'

'Dunno. Don't reckon.' Fab took a big drink. It looked like he was nearly done. 'Would be good if they did, but.'

Ben nodded. 'Who do you like then?'

'Out of the girls?'

'Yeah.'

'What's this? Twenty questions?' Fab smiled and threw a fistful of straw into the fire. It flared brightly and his face lit up like the devil. 'Bridie Flynn.'

'Bridie Flynn? Don't you reckon she's a bit fat?'

'Yeah, but big boobs.' Fab cupped his hands under his chest, to make sure Ben got the message. 'What about you? Who do you like?'

A strong gust of wind roared into the shed, flattening the fire and sending dust into their eyes.

'Jesus,' Fab said, wincing.

It was only a few seconds later that the rain came.

The fire fizzled and spat under the first heavy drops. They stood up with the sleeping bag and their cans and retreated deep inside the hay shed, the wind chasing them in. They went as far in as they could, right to the back wall, but the wind still whipped the rain in by their feet. Johnno stirred in his sleeping bag just a few metres away, only just out of the rain. It fell heavily on the steel roof in windy sheets and sounded like it might be hail. They couldn't see much outside, but could hear the trees bend and strain, the whoosh of cold air through wet leaves, and the crackle of small branches.

Ben tucked his jumper into his shorts. 'Jeez, it's gotten cold.'

'Yeah.' Fab's voice was a little shaky.

'Let's move up behind the hay bales.'

There was a big stack of bales on one side of the shed, but they didn't normally like going near it because Fab reckoned it was full of mice. Maybe rats too. Ben put his can on the ground, left Fab with the sleeping bag and climbed to the top, about five bales high. Once there, he moved two bales in front of him, building a small barrier to the wind and rain.

'C'mon,' he called down to Fab. 'It's better up here.'

* * *

As the wind tore in and rain hammered the roof, they were pleased with their hay-bale fortress.

'What were we talkin about?' Fab said.

'Girls. Bridie Flynn's boobs.'

'Wanna sip?' Fab held out the can toward him.

'Nah, you have it. I'll get mine in a sec.'

'I'll get it for ya then.'

'Nah, don't worry, I—' But Fab was up before he could finish, climbing over the hay-bale barrier. But he stopped suddenly halfway, straddling the bales, his body frozen.

'What's the matter?'

Ben stood up and saw what had made Fab freeze. In the distance, past the boundary fence and up the old highway, dim yellow headlights had appeared over the rise.

'Must be a farmer,' Ben said, but there was a shiver in his voice. Fab didn't answer. The highway bypass meant only locals used the road nowadays.

'Jeez, he's going slow.' Fab scratched his head. 'Like he's looking for something.'

He sat back down low and they both watched as the car crawled down the road, ever closer to the block. It was Ben who said it first.

'Reckon it could be Jimmy Shine?'

'Nah, how would he know?'

'Maybe he saw the fire.'

A sudden squall rushed the rain inside and they turned away, crouching lower behind the bales. When they turned back the car had stopped directly opposite, but still faced down the highway.

Then the headlights swung toward the gate.

'Shit!' Fab hissed. 'Quick, let's hide!'

'Should we wake Johnno?'

'Nah, bugger him. Let's get down behind the bales.'

They scurried down the back of the stack, sliding down the last few bales until their feet smacked on the concrete floor, their bodies sandwiched in the narrow space between the hay bales and the shed wall.

Ben closed his eyes. He was sure he could hear mice scurry against the steel of the shed. Something brushed his foot. He heard raw breaths and the rustle of the hay.

He opened his eyes to Fab inching slowly away from him.

'Where you goin?' Ben reached out and grabbed his arm.

Fab shook loose. 'Gonna have a look!' He crept to the corner of the stack and peered around the side.

'What d'ya see?'

Fab turned back and faced the shed wall. 'Nuthin. It's too dark.' His voice broke a little and Ben wondered if he was lying.

Ben squeezed his eyes shut again and wished the car away. He wished that the rain and the wind would stop. He wished they had never gone camping. But more than anything, he wished for home and he wished for his bed, to be safe and warm under his blankets.

Maybe it wasn't Jimmy Shine. Maybe it was just someone who was lost, or pulled over because of the weather. Maybe it was even his dad, come to pick them up because of all the rain.

Then, from somewhere out in the rain and the wind, he heard the heavy steel clap of a car door.

Ben felt a warm flood of piss run down his leg. He was suddenly conscious of the sound of his breath, more than any other time in his life. He tried to slow it, make it quieter, as though whoever was out there might hear him through the rain and the wind. He kept his body as still as he could, not wanting to rustle the hay at his back. Maybe if they both kept still enough and quiet enough, the car might just go away. As for Johnno, well—

Then, he heard footsteps.

Fab said, 'Fuck,' just once, only softly, like he didn't want Ben to hear.

They were heavy. Big shoes. Gumboots. Crunching and squelching through grass. But it was so loud with the rain and the wind that he—

Another clap of steel. The car boot. *Fuck*.

Ben opened his eyes as Fab moved slowly away once more.

'Where ya goin?' Hot tears stung Ben's eyes.

'Shut up!' Fab hissed. He moved to the corner of the bales and peered around the side.

'Oh Jesus,' he said.

'What?'

He turned back and grabbed Ben by the arm. 'It's goin! The car! It's goin!'

'Serious?'

'Serious!'

Ben didn't believe him, but then Fab proved it by going right out into full view and waving his arms around like a dick.

Ben wiped his cheeks and moved slowly out from behind the bales. The rain had begun to ease, but the wind still ripped across the paddock, creaking the trees. They both watched as the car drove out the gate, back up the highway and disappeared over the rise.

And Johnno kept snoring right through it all.

Ben and Fab sat beside what was left of the fire. It fizzled and smoked. They didn't drink any more of the beer and they didn't talk at all about who it might have been.

But they both agreed to stay awake til the sun came up. Just in case Jimmy Shine, or whoever it was, decided to come back.

Four

In the last week of school holidays, all the back-to-school ads were on telly – school shoes, pens, pencils and all that shit. Ben hated those ads because they reminded him of what was coming and gave him a sick feeling in his guts. This year he got it worse, mostly because Fab told him they would have Mr Burke again.

Ben hated Burke. He hated his fat guts, black beard and bald head, and the way his face would go all red when he talked. Ben could tell Mr Burke didn't like him either, by the way his lip curled when he said his name, like it was something disgusting. And he gave him bad marks on his stories, even though he'd always gotten good marks before.

He wagged a lot more than normal, pretending that he was sick so he could stay at home. Fab reckoned a headache was the best excuse, because no one could really tell if you had one or not. At first, when Ben tried it, his mum got the thermometer out and he thought he was done for. But she said he was a 'bit high' and never checked again after that.

Last year, Burke got him up the front of the class to explain why he missed so many days. After, when he was sent back to his desk, Fab passed him a note that said 'BURKE IS A CUNT'.

Ben wasn't sure what that meant, not exactly, but he agreed just the same.

* * *

In that last week of holidays, Ben wanted to stay close to home. He wanted to make every hour stretch out for as long as he could. He wanted to forget about the camping trip, the beers, and Jimmy Shine. He just wanted to play with Sunny. Ride his bike down Big Hill as fast as he could. Go down to the railway line and flatten some coins. Practise bike stunts at the block over the back and dig a hole as deep as he could. Have lunch every day at home with his mum – Strass sandwiches or alphabet soup.

The first time Ben saw the neighbour was in that last week. He wasn't spying on him or anything, just walking Sunny to the block over the back. He decided to take a shortcut down the lane between the witch's house and Daisy's old place. Fab reckoned that if you went too close to the witch's house she'd cast a spell, so Ben stuck close to the fence. The witch was a witch because she lived in a witch's house, with its peeling weatherboard, dark curtains and rusty iron roof.

He could see the top bit of the clothesline over the back fence of Daisy's old place. It was grey and ugly, spinning slowly in the wind with one brown towel strung from its lines. He remembered what Fab said about gob jobs and he thought, for no real reason at all, that it might be true.

'G'day mate.' Ben heard the man's voice before he saw him. It was low but cheery. A head popped up above the fence. He had dark skin and shiny black hair, but his eyes were weird looking.

'G'day.' Ben's voice sounded weak and girly and he hated it.

'I'm Ronnie.' The man dangled a long brown arm over the fence.

Ben reached up and shook his hand.

'Where you off to?' he said. Ben looked down and watched Sunny take a piss against the fence.

'Just goin to the block over the back.' Ben pulled at the lead and Sunny shot him a look.

'Fair enough. What's ya name, mate?'

'Ben.'

'Righto, Ben. Tell your dad I said g'day. All right?'

'Yep.' Ben yanked at Sunny and kept walking, with one eye still on the witch's house.

* * *

The block was behind Daisy's and the Pickerings' house. It was about three houses wide and, from it, Ben could see the shiny tin roof of his own house. Further beyond the block was the dirt road that led to the weedy paddock, and the railway line after that. The railway went all the way to Melbourne in one direction and to Adelaide in the other. The Overland train would sometimes come through, and him and Fab would wave at the passengers from the side of the tracks. Some of them would wave back, but most just slept right through.

The weedy paddock had a small dam, but there were no yabbies and it would dry up when it got really hot. That was where Joe, Daisy's brother, had built his cubbyhouse out of some old tin and two rotten timber pallets. He built it right next to the dam. When they found it, Ben and Fab smashed it to bits and threw the pieces of tin and timber in the water.

It was a really crap dam. They just didn't want Joe to think he could own it. It was mostly Fab's idea to smash it, though.

He felt bad in his guts when he thought about what

happened to Daisy and how Joe must have felt, and how the wrecked cubbyhouse probably made it worse. He knew that when the dam eventually dried up, they'd have to come and hide the tin and timber in the bushes, so no one would know.

He walked through the block, over the dirt road, and into the weedy paddock to check the dam. He picked up a stick on the way. Dad always said to carry a stick around there because there were snakes. The dam was about half full, enough to cover the cubbyhouse for a while yet. He would report that back to Fab, when he saw him at school. He would tell Mum too when he got home, but not about the cubbyhouse.

Ben walked back over the road to the block, thrusting the stick like a sword as he went. There were some old bricks stacked in one corner that had been there for years. At the start of the holidays, he'd decided to use them to build a jump for his BMX, but never got round to it. He'd seen a jump on *BMX Bandits* and he'd told Fab he'd make one just like it, so they could practise.

He let Sunny loose and carried some of the bricks to the middle of the block. He figured he would need some timber to make the ramp itself, but the brick structure would do for now. He was hungry, it was hot, and he could always finish it next weekend, especially if Fab helped him.

On the way back home he looked at the clothesline and wondered again if the man knew about what had happened there. None of the adults ever talked about it, or at least not that he'd heard. It was like they were pretending it never really happened. But he reckoned his dad might tell the man about it. Round the front he saw the man in the driveway with his blue car. He was cleaning the windows with a thick, wet sponge and Ben could see he was tall in his white singlet, his skin like chocolate in the hot sun. He wiped the rear window carefully with slow, wide strokes.

As Ben passed he stopped mid stroke, as though he sensed someone there.

He turned and waved at Ben with a smile, and Ben remembered that his name was Ronnie.

Five

B en could hear a steady beat outside. Clapping.
He was at the urinal taking a piss, but he could hear
it getting louder, faster. Like it was building up to something.

The school toilets were in a big tin shed at the edge of
the oval. They used to be in a different spot, up by the back
fence behind the classrooms, but some kid got fiddled by a
perve a few years back, so they shifted them further inside
the school.

Ben finished his piss before he was done properly, and he
felt his undies go wet. Just a bit though, not enough to show
through his shorts he didn't reckon.

It *was* clapping. Louder still. He rushed out of the toilet
shed, without washing his hands, to find out what was
happening.

The sun shone brightly and he squinted, shielding his eyes.
Down on the basketball court a circle had gathered. Grade
six boys and a few grade fives. A fight maybe? He could see
Johnno was there. And Pokey Stark. He could tell it was
Pokey because of the rat's tail.

It was only when he got close that he realised Fab was
in the middle of the circle. Ben put his hand on Johnno's
shoulder.

'What's goin on?'

Johnno turned with his big, stupid smile. 'It's Fab.'

'Yeah, I can see that.'

The clapping got faster, louder again. Fab slowly balanced himself on one foot, lifted the other off the ground, then raised both arms in the air. Ben recognised the pose right away.

The Crane.

Karate Kid.

Final scene.

'Get on with it, ya wog!' Pokey broke the circle and gave Fab a shove, sending him off balance.

The clapping stopped.

Ben pushed his way into the circle and shoved Pokey hard in the back. 'Leave him alone!'

Pokey turned to face him, eyes ablaze. 'The wog lover!'

'Get stuffed!'

Fab smiled at Ben and raised one foot off the ground.

Ben grabbed hold of his arm. 'What are you doin?'

Fab looked at him blankly.

'The wog reckons he's been doin karate over the holidays,' Pokey said. 'Says he's a black belt! He was just gonna show us his jump-kick, like Ralph Macho.'

'Macchio,' Ben said.

Pokey shrugged. 'Whatever.'

Ben glared at Fab.

Jesus Christ. Not again.

In grade three, Fab had pretended to be a professional break-dancer. Ben – of course – was part of his crew. It had taken two full years to live that down.

Ben turned back to Pokey. 'He's telling the truth. He's a black belt, all right?'

'Bull*shit*.' Pokey crossed his arms. 'He's gotta prove it. The greasy shit has to do his kick!' He spat at Ben's feet.

Ben shook his head. 'He won't do that kick. He won't do any kick.'

Fab looked at Ben, wide-eyed.

'See? I knew it was bullshit!' Pokey pointed at Fab, right up close in his face. 'Now you're a wog *and* a liar!'

Everyone fell silent. It suddenly felt like the whole school was watching.

Ben shook his head. 'Nah, you've got it all wrong. He *can* do it. He's just not *allowed* to. The sensei forbids it.'

Ben then did his best, and only, impression of a Japanese accent. '*You must only use karate in the defence of self.*'

Pokey's face went red and he gave Fab another shove. 'I'll give you a reason later!' He glared at Ben. 'When your boyfriend isn't around.'

* * *

Ben and Fab headed back toward the classrooms, walking quickly across the hot asphalt, threading their way through skipping girls and the nerds swapping comic books.

Fab laughed. 'What's so funny?'

'That look on Pokey's face, when you did the *Monkey Magic* thing.'

'It wasn't *Monkey Magic*. It was Mr Miyagi.'

'Really? It sounded like Monkey. Or Pigsy.'

'It was Miyagi.'

'Same diff.'

Ben felt his face go hot – he grabbed Fab by his t-shirt. 'Why do you do shit like that? You're asking for trouble, y'know? Ya can't just expect me to jump in all the time.'

Fab shook his head. 'I had to get him off my back.'

'And that's your best idea?'

'Planned it over the holidays.'

'Over the whole holidays?'

'The last day.'

'Why didn't ya tell me?'

Fab put his hands together and bowed. '*Element of surprise, young master*. I could have done the kick though.' He thrust one leg out.

'Really.'

'I've been practising. Got the *Karate Kid* video and everything.'

'Any other moves?'

'Nah, that's it.'

'Not much for a black belt, is it?'

He shrugged. 'Probably didn't think it through.'

There was a short queue at the bubble-taps – a few nervous preps and one of the retarded kids, the Down syndrome one. There were two retarded kids at school. They both came every second day on the vegie bus from the Special School.

Ben leaned over the trough and took a long drink. The water was warm at first, but started to cool after a bit. Fab slurped noisily at the tap next to him. There was only ever enough pressure for one tap to work properly.

Ben straightened up and wiped his mouth. 'So, what are you gonna do now?'

The Down syndrome kid suddenly started crying for no reason, which made one of the preps start too.

Fab lifted his mouth from the tap. 'What d'ya mean? Bell's about to go.'

Ben shook his head. 'About Pokey. He'll be gunning for ya.'

Fab looked up, the water running down his chin and onto his t-shirt. His hand was still on the tap – he kept it running. His lip quivered just a little, then stopped, but Ben noticed it.

'He'll pick on me anyway. No matter what I do,' Fab said. He swallowed and wiped his mouth with the back of his hand. 'It's just the way it is.'

Fab was wearing the same blue t-shirt that he'd been wearing in summer for two years. A lot of his clothes were his cousin's old stuff. This t-shirt had been too small last year, and was even worse now; tight at the shoulders and riding up over his belly, with a strip of downy brown skin showing above his shorts. He looked like a skinny rabbit dressed up by a little kid, standing there in the sun with big, shiny eyes.

And for the first time in his life, though he would never admit it to himself or anyone else, Ben felt like hugging him.

Fab slapped him on the shoulder. 'Anyway, Pokey might be after you instead.' He laughed after he said it, but Ben could tell he forced it out. 'Maybe I teach you my ancient wisdom, young master.'

He bowed, Jap-style, squinting his eyes.

'*Wax-on... Wax-off. Young master. Wax-on... Wax-off.*'

Six

Apart from the karate incident, school had been okay for the first two weeks; grade six was mostly like grade five and Ben was happy that Fab was in his class. Pokey had been yelling shit out in the yard, but he hadn't done anything. Not yet anyway.

The best bit of school so far was that Mr Burke had been sick the second week, so they had a substitute teacher – Miss Feely from Ballarat. She was much nicer than Burke. She used coloured chalk and wore very thin summer dresses with flowers on them. Fab reckoned she had really nice boobs. 'Banana tits,' he said. He reckoned he'd seen her at the pool on the weekend in a bikini. Ben thought Fab was probably lying about that, but he didn't say so. But he really hoped Burke might be properly sick. Like cancer or maybe AIDS.

On the Saturday of the second week, Ben spent the morning watching cartoons. His dad was at work and his mum had gone shopping. Halfway through *The Jetsons* he went for a piss while the ads were on.

Then, from the bathroom, he heard a loud knock on the door.

He finished his piss against the bowl, avoiding the splash of the water, and decided not to flush the toilet. He'd just wait, stay quiet and pretend no one was home. The car wasn't there, so there's no way they would know. And he wasn't that worried about missing the rest of *The Jetsons* – it was usually pretty crap.

Ben never liked it when his parents had visitors. He liked it when it was just him and them; when other people came around he wasn't sure how to act anymore. Sometimes he tried to be like an adult, asking questions and that, but it made him feel weird. Mostly, he tried to stay in his room.

The worst bit was the knock on the door. The door had a wooden frame and yellow patterned glass and when people knocked it was really loud – you could hear it anywhere in the house, even the backyard. Through the yellow glass, he could make out their body shape and would try to guess who it was before he answered.

The ones that came the most were the Chappels, a couple from down the street. Des had fought in the war and looked much older than Ben's parents, with grey hair and thick black eyebrows. He smelled like gum trees sometimes, then other times like rubber. His wife, Roma, smoked non-stop and had short white hair, wiry like a fox terrier. She wore soft woolly jumpers. Ben's mum said they were mohair, or maybe cashmere, but he didn't know what either of those was.

Sometimes they went to the Chappels' place, which was a neat, white weatherboard his mum told him to be 'careful' in. Ben hated going there – he'd be stuck for hours while they talked about politics and it was so boring. They had a telly but it was about a hundred years old and was never turned on. He wasn't allowed to do anything because everything was really clean and his mum said the Chappels would notice if anything was out of place.

There was also the Jacks. They didn't come as much as the Chappels because they lived on a farm. Barry Jack was a big farmer with a really loud laugh. He used to be married to Dolly Jack, who Ben never met, but he heard his mum say that she left him because of his drinking. Once he gave up booze she said he was too boring, so she moved to Mildura to live with some bloke called Fred. Ben had never seen Fred, but he had a moustache that Ben's mum said was 'disgusting'.

Barry Jack looked like he could be in the Wild West, a tall cowboy with long, bushy sideburns. After Dolly left, he got a Filipina bride from one of the classified ads in the *Aussie Post* and they had three boys together.

Ben liked the *Aussie Post* because it had the Ettamogah Pub and pictures of girls in bikinis. He also liked when the Jack boys came around because they'd play cricket and he got to bat for nearly the whole time. They were pretty hopeless.

Then there was Alan Bulger, or 'Bulger' as his dad called him. He lived over the road with his parents in a big old brick house with no fences. He was a bit fat and he had thick glasses that made his eyes look big. He seemed much younger than Mum and Dad and he always stayed too long and drank a lot of beer. Mum would always end up telling him how he should try to find a wife. Ben didn't like him much because he looked at him kind of funny, but Mum reckoned it was because he had a lazy eye.

Then there was Uncle Ray, his dad's brother. He ran a pool hall in Melbourne, had a thick beard like Brutus and drove a black Celica. It was the coolest car Ben had ever seen, with a sunroof and everything – like Kitt from *Knight Rider*. Ray didn't come much though and Ben's mum said he would only ever come 'if he wants something'.

Last time, he brought a girlfriend with long blonde hair and a really short skirt. Her name was Lisa. Mum went all stiff around her and talked like she was a school teacher.

That night, Ben wanked quietly in his bed, thinking about Lisa's short skirt and what might be underneath, while she sat in the kitchen with Mum and Dad and Ray, talking about why Bob Hawke had started crying.

He couldn't look her or Uncle Ray in the eyes after that.

* * *

After a minute, the knocking stopped. He stuck his head out from the bathroom and looked down the hallway to the front door, but there was no shadow behind the glass. The quiet piss technique had worked – they were gone.

He was in the hallway when he heard the knock again, louder this time. He glanced at the front but there was still no one there.

Then, he realised – it was the side door. *Shit.*

Only family used the side door, which opened straight into the lounge from the driveway, so it was weird that someone would be knocking there. It was a sliding door, but it had the same yellow glass as the front and was right next to the telly. Whoever was there would know it was turned on, because Ben liked it loud, especially when his parents weren't home.

He stepped quietly into the lounge and saw a tall, dark figure shimmer through the glass. It was Barry Jack for sure. Maybe he was knocking on the side because he thought they were out back.

Ben unclipped the latch and slid the door open with a metal squeal. But he could tell right away that it wasn't Barry Jack, because he was wearing shorts. Barry Jack never wore shorts. Neither did cowboys, come to think of it.

A tall, muscular man in a white singlet and bright blue stubbie shorts stood outside, with one hand on his hip and his other arm angled above the door. It was Ronnie, the new neighbour from up the road, and he had a big smile on his face.

'G'day, mate. Ben, wasn't it? Ya dad home?'

Ben shielded his eyes from the sun. Ronnie seemed bigger up close, his shoulders wide and the veins in his arms stuck out, blue and green. His hands were enormous, red and knotty. He looked strong. Stronger than his dad. Stronger than Barry Jack. Maybe even stronger than Fab's dad.

'Nah, he's at work.'

'Ya mum?'

'Shopping.'

'Ah, no worries. I'll come back a bit later then.' He was wearing the same singlet as the other day and Ben noticed some stains on it, down near his belly. Even though he said he'd come back later, he kept standing there. He kept smiling too and Ben saw how his teeth were kind of brown and sharp looking. Funny angles. Crooked. It felt a bit weird, standing there in the doorway, with Ronnie smiling at him.

After what seemed like forever, Ronnie asked him how school was going. Ben said it was good and Ronnie got out a pack of smokes from his back pocket. The pack was soft, like it was made from paper, not cardboard – Ben had never seen one like it. He lit a cigarette and blew the smoke high in the air above him.

'Have you seen anyone blow smoke rings before?' he said.

'Nah, not for real or anything,' Ben said.

Ben had only ever seen it in cartoons. Popeye did it sometimes with his pipe. Roma Chappel smoked all the time but never blew rings; she was always just clouded in blue smoke that smelled kind of minty. 'Bloody menthol,' Mum would say, and after she double-checked their car was gone, she would open all the windows.

Ronnie took a deep drag, then made his lips go kind of weird like a fish as three rings of smoke popped out, like they came from down his throat. He coughed a little, then laughed. Ben smiled and nodded, 'Cool.' He wasn't sure what else to say. He really just wanted to shut the door and go back inside before *Scooby-Doo* started. He was hungry and had planned to make a cheese and tomato toastie.

Ronnie reached into his pocket. 'Wanna see my lighter?'

'Okay.'

Ronnie showed it to him. It was a white one, but with a girl in a red bikini on one side, just like the girls from the *Aussie Post*.

Ronnie smiled. 'You like it?'

'Yeah.'

'She's all right, isn't she?'

Ben nodded.

Ronnie started asking more questions, like if he had many friends. Ben told him about Fab, but it didn't seem like Ronnie listened, because he asked him the same question again not long after. Then he asked him if he had a girlfriend. Ben's face went hot.

'Nah.' He shook his head.

'You like girls, though?'

Ben looked down at Ronnie's feet. He had black rubber thongs on. And his feet were really long.

He shrugged. 'Yeah, course I do.'

Ronnie laughed a bit. 'That's good then. So have you got a job, like a paper round or anything?'

'Nah, Mum reckons I'm too young.'

He wondered if he should ask him something back, like he saw his parents do. His mum told him he should talk to adults – '*Be a polite young man*' – she said. But Ronnie just kept talking and asking questions. Ben noticed sweat forming in small drops on his forehead as he stood there in the sun with his dark skin. He wasn't black like an Abo or anything, but more a deep brown like the surfers Ben saw on *Wide World of Sports*. Like Tom Curren, or even Sunny Garcia, but more Aussie looking.

He told Ben that he didn't have a girlfriend either, and then the smile kind of dropped from his face. 'They're mostly trouble, mate,' he said. 'Only good for one thing.'

Ben could hear the music start for *Scooby-Doo*. Ronnie finally finished his smoke and crushed it against the brick wall. 'Good talkin to ya, Ben,' he said, and he winked. 'Tell ya folks I'll be back later, all right?'

Ben nodded. Ronnie walked back down the driveway, his big feet and thongs slapping the concrete as he went. Ben went back inside and got the jaffle maker out from the cupboard, but decided to wait til the ads came on.

* * *

Ronnie came back late in the afternoon, an hour or so after Ben's dad got home from work. He wasn't wearing his singlet, but a green short-sleeved shirt with the yellow logo of the goldmine – a man swinging a pick. Mum got beers and they sat in the kitchen, so Ben went to his bedroom to read comics. He'd just got the latest *2000 AD* from the newsagent.

It took ages for Ronnie to leave. A couple of times it sounded like he was about to go, but then Ben's dad got him another beer. Ben quietly cursed his dad for making him stay. In the end, he heard his mum invite him for dinner, but Ronnie said he had to go.

'Got an early start,' he said. His voice was loud and a bit rough and Ben was happy he was finally leaving.

* * *

At dinnertime, his dad told him the news – Ronnie had a job for him.

'Just mow the lawns once a fortnight and a few odd chores.' Ben's dad kept his eyes on the telly as he spoke. It was highlights of the West Indies tour of Australia – a day-nighter at the MCG. Dean Jones was in.

'Ten bucks if you do it right.' His dad had this way of asking and telling at the same time.

Dean Jones made it to forty, so Viv Richards put Curtly

Ambrose back on to bowl. Then Ben's mum got the ice-cream from the freezer and said what a nice man Ronnie was.

'So charming,' she said.

Ben didn't really feel like he could say no after that.

Seven

B en wasn't sure whether to knock. He tried the doorbell first, but he couldn't hear it ring. Maybe it wasn't working. Or maybe they'd gone out. It was Sunday, so maybe they all did something together that he didn't know about. Maybe he should just go home.

He decided to wait for another ten seconds. He counted them quickly under his breath, *five... six... seven... eight... nine* and—

He heard footsteps coming fast down the hallway.

'Ben!'

It was Fab's mum. Ben's thoughts went right away to her pantyhose and the dark patch in the middle.

'I am sorry,' she said, holding the door open, 'I had the fan on and couldn't hear a thing!'

'Hello, Mrs Morressi.' He said it in a sing-song way, like a prep saying good morning to the teacher. It made him cringe inside.

'Please, Ben. Call me Eva.'

Ben felt his cheeks go hot. *Eva.*

She stepped to one side of the doorway, 'Come in, come in.'

She wasn't wearing the pantyhose, her legs were bare, but she had a green skirt that swooshed as he passed. She smelled like flowers and the air was somehow cooler by her side. She didn't have any shoes on and her toenails were painted dark and shiny. She had bright red lipstick and big eyes. Ben's heart was jumping all over the place.

'Fab, he is out back. He's been waiting for you.'

The house was gloomy and almost cold inside. It was a big place, a weatherboard. 'A rambling old joint,' his dad had said. It was on Seaby Street, which Mum said was the nicest street in town, running from Main Street all the way to the highway. His mum said the mayor, the surgeon and both the lawyers lived in Seaby Street. All the big, old houses were there. Dad reckoned that Fab's dad could only buy a place on Seaby Street because of the insurance job. Ben didn't ask again what that meant. He decided it probably wasn't important.

'You like a drink?' Mrs Morressi touched Ben's shoulder and it was like a lightning bolt straight through him.

'Ah... nah. I mean, no thank you. I'll just go out back and...'

'Yes, yes, Fabri. He is out back.' She smiled and walked into the kitchen. 'You go play the crickets, yes. I make you both nice lunch after.'

Ben stopped at the back door and watched again the way her skirt brushed against her legs. She had light brown skin, smooth and lovely. He wondered what underwear she might have on. And if she had a matching bra. Maybe a lacy one. Definitely a lacy one and—

'Ben? Are you all right?' She frowned, her lips pursed. 'Are you sure you don't want a drink? You look a little pale.'

'No, thanks. I... um... I better go outside and see Fab.'

She nodded and smiled, all big shining eyes and white teeth and bright red lips like a movie star.

Jesus.

If Fab's dad – or his father, or whatever – if he knew what Ben was thinking, he'd slice his throat right open with that huge hunting knife. Just the thought of him sent a chill through Ben's bones.

He hoped like hell that Fab was out the back on his own, that his father wasn't there too. He hoped he'd gone into work and wasn't home, even though he normally did the night shift. Maybe he wouldn't be home all day. It would just be him, Fab and Mrs Morressi. Fab and his mum. Fab and Eva.

Eva.

He suddenly realised he didn't even know Fab's father's name. Truth was, he didn't really want to. But he imagined it would be something scary. Like Victor or Ivan. Or maybe Boris.

* * *

From the back door, there was a winding, half-rotten, timber ramp that led down to the yard. A wide driveway snaked down the right side of the house and through the yard, leading to a large, open-walled garage.

From the doorway, Ben could see there was no Kingswood parked inside, just the Pacer, which meant Fab's dad probably wasn't home. He moved quickly down the ramp to a small patch of dry grass. Fab was sitting there, with their dog, Sofia.

'Hey!'

Fab looked up. 'Didn't think you were coming.'

'I told ya I was.'

'Yeah, but last time...'

'I had to help Dad last time, remember?'

That was bullshit. Though it hurt him to do it, he usually made up an excuse if Fab asked him over.

Ben gave Sofia a pat. She was an old, black labrador. She was a pretty boring dog, just sat around most of the time. And she stank. They used to have a super-smart kelpie called Tippy, but Fab's dad shot him when he got a bit sick once. Fab said his father didn't believe in vets. They had a cocky too, Niccolo, but he was round the back of the garage and you never saw him, though you'd hear him scream out like a mental case sometimes.

'What do ya wanna do?' Fab said.

'Dunno. Cricket?'

Fab was up on his feet as soon as Ben said it. He already had it all set up.

The rules were pretty simple.

At the bottom end of the driveway was an upturned trampoline – that was the automatic wicketkeeper. An old steel rubbish bin, in front of the trampoline, was the stumps.

If you nicked the ball and it hit the trampoline, you were out (even down the leg-side, which was a new rule). Over the fence on the full was out, and you had to go get it. If you hit the house on the full, you were out too. One-hand-one-bounce was out, but there was no LBW – it caused too many arguments.

Hitting the house along the ground was four runs. The garage on the full was out. Garage along the ground was two runs. Hitting the side fence was a single.

And you couldn't get out first ball.

Ben picked up a tennis ball. 'You gonna bat?'

Fab smiled. 'Course.' Home team always batted first. Fab was usually the West Indies, while Ben was Australia. Fab reckoned the Australian team was full of wankers and Ben kind of agreed with him about that. He liked Merv Hughes, but.

Ben walked back up the driveway to mark out his run-up. Sofia followed him, slobbering and wagging her fat, smelly tail.

'Where's ya dad?' he said.

Fab picked up his bat, an old Duncan Fearnley, and marked out the crease with his foot. 'He's gone to Sid's.'

Ben's chest relaxed a little. He nodded, pretending not to care. 'Fair enough.'

Thing was, he was hardly ever invited around if Fab's dad was there anyway. He didn't know if it was because Fab's dad didn't like him, or if Fab was embarrassed. Either way, Ben preferred it. It was better with just Mrs Morressi. Even more so lately. Much better just with her. With Eva. *Eva*. Such a nice name.

Fab made it to thirty-two before Ben got him. Caught behind, down the leg-side. Ben was happy to get him for less than fifty and he could tell Fab was pissed off, especially for getting out with the new rule.

'Well-batted,' Ben said.

'Thanks.' Fab handed over the bat, but didn't look at him, which confirmed he was angry.

The handle felt sweaty. The rubber had worn through ages ago and Fab had patched it with electrical tape. Ben marked out his own crease, a little further out than Fab's, because Fab always bowled a bit too short.

'Have you seen Jimmy Shine around?' Ben said.

'You mean since...'

'Yeah.'

'Nah. Probably got his fill that night. Good wanking material.'

Ben laughed. 'Probably.'

He only got to face five balls before Fab's mum called out that lunch was ready. He was on eleven not out.

* * *

It was like nothing Ben had ever tasted before. The sauce was rich and thick and it was just unbelievable. Fab's mum grated some weird hard cheese to go on top – she didn't just use the bag stuff like Ben's mum did. His dad called the bag cheese 'the sawdust' and thought it was pretty funny.

Fab's mum said the cheese was 'Parmigiano' that she got in Ballarat. She even drank some red wine in a normal glass, not like the tall dusty ones his mum kept in the special room. She drank wine in the middle of the day, just with him and Fab, like they were all adults or something.

Fab's mum was from another planet. A much better planet.

'This is really nice, Mrs Morressi.' He couldn't bring himself to say Eva, especially in front of Fab, but he snuck a look at her chest as he said it. She had a grey t-shirt on, with a couple of buttons that were open near the collar. Her boobs weren't huge or anything, but they were a nice round shape. Much rounder than his mum's ones, not that he looked at them. But he'd noticed that his mum's were a bit pointy, a bit like Miss Feely's. He saw them once, just in a bra, and they were bigger than he expected.

'*Grazie*... I mean, thank you, Ben.' She smiled with those big red lips. 'I cook the sauce for three hours, you know? Does your mum make the bolognese?' She didn't even say it like his mum did, it was more like 'bolo-nezzy', and her tongue rolled a bit at the end.

'Yeah, but nothing like this. She just fries a packet of mince in a pan and puts a jar of something in it. Dolmio, I think it's called.'

Mrs Morressi clicked her tongue. 'That is not my way,' she said. 'But,' she shrugged, 'everyone can do things differently, no?'

Ben smiled. She had this way of saying no when she meant yes. Of saying things like they were questions, even when they weren't. And Ben decided right then that she was just about the nicest lady in the world.

Then the front door squeaked open. And it was like all the air got sucked right out of the room.

They all stopped eating. Ben shot a look at Fab, who placed his fork down slowly.

Fab's mum was up like a shot. She got a big bowl from the cupboard and started piling it with spaghetti. There were heavy footsteps down the hallway. Really heavy. Fab stared straight down into his bowl and Ben could tell he was gritting his teeth by the way his cheeks shook a bit.

'*Buongiorno!*' Fab's mum called out really loud. 'I cook you pasta! You eat?'

The footsteps stopped. Ben turned around and there he was, standing in the lounge room like a mountain. He was swaying a bit and he wiped his mouth with his sleeve. He was holding a bottle in a brown paper bag. He coughed. His eyes were wild and bright, but rolling around a bit like he was crazy. He didn't even look at Ben. Or Fab.

'*Buonanotte!*' he said, then he laughed loudly and staggered into a bedroom, slamming the door behind him.

Mrs Morressi didn't answer him, but picked up Fab and Ben's plates, even though they hadn't finished.

'You boys go outside and keep playing the crickets, yes?' She smiled at Ben, but it was different this time. Thinner and smaller. Like it didn't quite reach her eyes.

* * *

Fab was batting again before long. Ben was out for seventeen. One-hand-one-bounce. 'Second innings then,' he said.

Ben was getting tired. The pasta was delicious. He just needed some more of it. He took a breather, sitting on the grass with Sofia.

'So, has Pokey given you any more trouble?' he said.

Fab smiled. 'Don't worry about Pokey.' He leaned the bat against the rubbish bin. 'I've got a plan.'

Ben shook his head. 'Jesus, Fab. You and your plans. Why don't you just tell your parents or something?'

He glanced up to the house. 'What are they gonna do?'

Ben shrugged.

'Nah, I got it all sorted. You know how he rides his bike up the hill to school?'

'Yeah.'

'Well...' he grinned like a cat. 'Never mind.'

Ben stood up. 'C'mon, tell me.'

'Nah, you'll have to wait and see.'

'Well, if you don't tell me, don't expect me to jump in when it all goes to shit.'

Fab nodded, but they both knew Ben didn't mean it. He picked up the bat. 'C'mon, go bowl, will ya.'

'Why don't ya just keep a low profile. Avoid him.'

'It's all right for you to say that. You don't know what it's like.'

'I do know what it's—'

'Nah, it's all right for you.' Fab shook his head. 'You're one of them. I mean, you're not *like* them... you're my friend. But I'm a wog.' He winced a little at the word. 'It's always gonna be like that.'

'I'm not one of them, though. And it won't always be like this.' He had no idea if the second bit was true.

Fab took his stance, whacking the bat three times on the crease. 'I'm sick of talking about it. Just go bowl, will ya.'

Ben went back to his run-up. He wasn't the quickest of bowlers. Steven Troeth at school had that crown. But he was accurate, just short of a good length and pitched outside off-stump. Predictable and dependable.

To a fault, as it turned out.

On the first ball of the third over after lunch, Fab danced forward and clipped it crisply from his toes, sending it over Ben's head and straight through a large sash window. They both watched in silent horror as the glass collapsed and jagged shards crashed to the ground. Sofia, who was asleep on the grass, yelped and ran up the driveway as quickly as Ben had ever seen.

It all happened so fast after that.

Fab stood still, wide-eyed and stunned. Ben ran down the driveway and wrenched the bat from his hands.

Mrs Morressi came out first, her big Italian eyes like shiny saucers. She rushed down the timber ramp, her hands slapping at her cheeks, her mouth going for air like a goldfish.

'I did it, Mrs Morressi. I did it!' Ben said. 'I'm sorry!'

But it didn't make any difference.

There was a side door that opened out onto the driveway. Ben had never known about it until then, until Fab's father came running out.

He was wearing white underpants and was yelling something in Italian as he ran down the driveway. He was enormous and hairy and he was swinging a thick leather belt with a big brass buckle. Fab was already crying.

'I did it, Mr Morressi.' Ben said. '*I did it!*'

Mr Morressi didn't look like he heard what Ben said and he grabbed Fab by the arm. Mrs Morressi wasn't Eva anymore and she was yelling in Italian, but he didn't hear her either.

He started to whip Fab with the leather belt, with the buckle and everything. Mrs Morressi grabbed his arm, but he turned and started whipping her too.

And that's when Ben found out Fab's father's name, even though he never wanted to know.

'Gustavo! No, please! Gustavo!'

Ben dropped the bat and ran up the driveway. He ran up the driveway as fast as he could, and out into the street.

All the way home he ran, and all the way he could feel his heart pounding and hear the blood rushing in his ears.

And even when he got home, ran inside his room and buried his head under his pillow, he was sure he could still hear Fab screaming.

Eight

The first time Ben went to Ronnie's house was to cut the grass. It was Saturday and he played cricket in the morning at Great Western and they won. He'd given up playing tennis on Saturdays; it clashed with cricket and he liked cricket better because Fab and him were on the same team.

He'd liked looking at the girls at tennis too, so it wasn't an easy choice. His mum wasn't happy about him choosing cricket – she said tennis was a nicer sport and there was more money in it.

Fab reckoned tennis was for 'toffs'. When Ben asked him what that meant, he said it was for rich kids. Ben reckoned the real reason Fab didn't like tennis was because it was the one sport he was really shithouse at. But he didn't say anything about it.

When Ben got home after cricket, his mum told him Ronnie had come by and he'd have to go over there after lunch. Ben didn't want to go, but he didn't say anything. It wasn't like he could get out of it. If he tried, he knew his dad would be furious.

Still, if he got it done quick he might get some time in the arvo, maybe see what Fab was doing. Plus, the ten bucks would be handy. Sportspower had just got the new Nike Air Max.

* * *

When he got there, Ronnie was in the driveway, bent over the mower with a toolbox on the concrete beside him. He was wearing long grey pants, the ones with pockets about halfway down. He had the green mining shirt on and big black leather boots that looked like they had steel caps.

Ben hoped the mower might be broken. Ronnie turned his head as the gate squeaked open, his face red and sweaty, eyes squinting into the sun.

'G'day Ben.'

'Hi...' He cleared his throat. 'G'day.'

'Just changin the spark plug over for ya.' Ronnie stood up, his hands on his hips.

Ben didn't know what a spark plug was. 'Thanks,' he said.

Ronnie pulled out a smoke from his shirt pocket and lit it with a big silver lighter, which he clipped shut with a thwack. Ben wondered what happened to the other lighter, or if maybe Ronnie had a collection of them. Maybe different girls in bikinis.

He looked at the lawn; it was about half a foot long in parts, but had longer bits where tall, skinny yellow flowers had shot up. He didn't think it would take him very long. He looked back at Ronnie, who was watching his eyes.

'Ya gotta do here and out the back. Just a couple of hours, I reckon.' He drew back hard on his cigarette. He looked almost shiny in the sun, like marble, his forearms mapped with thick veins. 'I'll finish this,' he nodded at his smoke, 'and I'll start it up for ya.' A smile started at the corner of his mouth, but stayed there.

Ben didn't know there was grass out back. He'd always thought the clothesline would be set in concrete and that's as far as his imagination got before Daisy took over. He shuddered at the thought of mowing the grass out there, with the clothesline spinning behind him. He might look around and there she'd be, swinging with her rotting white face and dead eyes.

Ronnie flicked his cigarette onto the driveway, reached down to the starter cord and tore the machine to life.

* * *

Ben was about halfway through mowing out front when Fab skidded up the driveway on his bike.

'Whatcha doin?'

'What?' Ben yelled over the mower.

'Whatcha doin?'

'What? I can't hear ya!'

'Turn it off!'

'What?'

Fab pointed at the throttle. 'Turn it off!' He leaned over and pulled at the lever. The mower spluttered to a stop.

'Started your new job?' he said. 'Ya mum just told me.'

'Yeah.' Ben lifted his t-shirt and wiped the sweat from his face.

'Where's ya boss?'

'Dunno. In the house I think.' Ben nodded at Fab's bike. 'You fix the buckled wheel?'

Fab shrugged. 'You did well today. How many wickets was it?'

'Three,' Ben said. 'You did well too. Took that catch.'

'Yeah, Halls Gap are shit though. We've got Swifts next week, they're top of the ladder.'

'Did ya mum pick ya up after?'

Fab adjusted the grip on his handlebars. 'Yep.'

It was the first time Ben had mentioned anything about Fab's parents since last weekend. Fab hadn't said anything about it at school. And neither had Ben. Not to each other or anyone else. It was a silent agreement to pretend nothing happened. Same as last time.

It was just easier that way. Ben could tell that Fab never wanted to talk about it, not directly. And neither did he.

Some of the other kids asked Fab why he wore trousers all week, even though it was hot. So Ben wore trousers on Thursday and Friday too, just so they would shut up about it.

'Gonna go yabbying later,' Fab said. 'Reckon you can come?'

He shrugged. 'Dunno. Gotta do the back too.'

'Really?' Fab raised his eyebrows. 'You better watch out for you-know-who then.'

'Get stuffed, will ya?' Ben reached down for the starter cord.

'Might see you later then, if you make it out alive. Near the Leviathan again, all right?'

'Yep.'

As Fab pushed off down the driveway, Ben looked back to the house and saw the curtains of the front window shake for just a second, and then close.

* * *

When Ben finished the front, Ronnie came out and stood on the porch, surveying the yard. He'd changed his clothes and was wearing green shorts and a clean white singlet. He looked clean too, like he'd just had a shower, his shiny black hair neatly combed to one side.

'Ready to do the back then?'

'Yep.' Ben pushed the mower onto the cement driveway. He could feel the heat through the thin rubber soles of his runners. They were Dunlop KT-26's his mum had bought for him; they were pretty shit and cheap as. It would be great to get the Nikes, especially before Shane or anyone else got them. He knew Fab would never get them. The Morressis couldn't afford stuff like that.

'I'll get ya a drink and meet ya round the rear.' Ronnie smiled and disappeared back inside.

* * *

The backyard was smaller than he had imagined, with a tin shed in one corner. The galvanised steel clothesline was in the middle, at the end of a narrow strip of concrete that led from the back step. The rest of it was grass, same length as the front.

Ben was determined not to get spooked. He turned and concentrated on the house, looking closely at the weatherboard, the guttering, and the back door. He tried not to think about her. Then Ronnie appeared behind the flywire and swung it open with a tinny screech.

'You all right mate? You look a bit pale.' He handed Ben a can of Mello Yello. It was really cold, like it had been in the freezer.

'Yep, just a bit hot.' Ben cracked the can, closed his eyes and let the sweet lemon wash down his throat. He winced as it gave him brain freeze.

'It's hot all right.' Ronnie looked up at the clear sky, then went quiet for a second. 'You can take off your top if ya want. No one will see ya out here.' Ronnie smiled and looked at Ben right in the eyes. Then he frowned a little, like he was concentrating.

'Nah,' Ben shook his head, 'I'll be right.' He had a bit of a belly, so he didn't like taking his top off, even when he was yabbying just with Fab.

'Up to you, mate. I might though, pretty warm.' Ronnie stepped down onto the grass, peeled off his white singlet, and sat down on the step. Ben noticed how his stomach rippled and his chest was big and wide, with thin veins running through it, like it was all muscle and no fat. A bit like Arnold Schwarzenegger in *The Terminator*, but not as big. Ronnie's skin was lighter where the singlet was, but still browner than a normal person's.

Ben drank deeply from the can, right to the bottom.

'Jeez, mate, you were thirsty.' Ronnie reached out for the empty. His long, thick fingers were cool against Ben's hot hands.

'Thanks,' Ben said, his gaze returning to the mower.

'Good to be outside, isn't it?'

'Yeah.'

Ronnie looked up at the sky. 'I'm down that bloody mine most of the time. Just drilling all day long. Mud, rock and a bunch of sweaty blokes. Good to get a bit of sun now and again.' He shielded his eyes. 'Gets pretty lonely down there too.' He looked at Ben and smiled. 'Nice to have some company, isn't it?'

Ben nodded. 'I spose.'

'Don't get me wrong, but. The boys down the mine are all right.' He squashed the can in his hands and got a big smile on his face. 'They're just a bit wild. Who knows? Maybe you'll meet em sometime.'

Ben nodded. 'Yep.'

'How was cricket anyway?'

'Good, we won.'

'Nice one! Ya mum tells me you're a pretty flash bowler.' Ronnie smiled.

Ben was surprised his mum had mentioned it, but he felt a wave of pride flow through him. 'I'm all right.'

'Nah, mate, she said you're very good. Bet the girls are impressed.'

'I dunno.' Ben smiled and shook his head. Ronnie bounced the crushed can from one hand to the other.

'Yeah, I reckon they would be impressed. Good lookin boy like you.'

'I dunno.' Ben felt his face go hot and he stared at the lawn-mower, quietly willing it back to life.

Ronnie stopped bouncing the can. 'You like girls, don't ya?' he said, more softly.

'Yeah, I spose.'

'You spose?' Ronnie laughed. 'Well, I've got some mags I can give ya next time, kinda like a bonus.' Ben looked at him and Ronnie winked. 'Just don't tell ya mum. Our secret, yeah?'

Ben looked back at the mower. 'Yep.'

'I'll get that thing going for ya, mate.' Ronnie put his hand on Ben's shoulder, then softly brushed Ben's cheek with his fingertips, before leaning down for the starter cord. As he came in close, Ben could smell his breath and it was funny and sweet.

The mower roared back to life and Ronnie stood there grinning, with his hands on his hips.

And Ben had forgotten all about Daisy and the clothesline.

Nine

Fab disappeared at lunchtime.

They'd been playing bat tennis with Johnno and Shane. It was doubles, so without Fab it was pretty useless. He said he was going to get a drink, but he'd been gone ages.

Ben wouldn't normally have been worried, but there was Pokey to consider. He knew as long as Fab stuck with him, nothing would happen. Pokey was dumb as dog shit, but smart enough to know that Ben would beat him in a fight.

Fab was wiry and strong, but he was short and didn't have much reach. He could handle himself against some kids, but Pokey was a lot bigger. Plus, Pokey had friends and Fab didn't. Well, he had one, but that didn't count for much if Ben wasn't there.

Pokey had one other thing that Fab didn't have – a pocketknife. He carried it everywhere, a fold-up one with a bone-coloured handle. He reckoned his dad, who lived in Geelong, gave it to him. When Ben asked his dad if he could have one too, he said that Pokey's dad was in jail and that should tell him everything he needed to know about knives.

Ben dropped his bat on the asphalt. 'I better go look for him.'

'So Pokey's right,' Johnno said. 'You *are* his boyfriend.'

Ben glared. 'You're such an in-bred, Johnno.'

'What?'

'Hasn't your mum told ya? What are you gonna call your brother? Dad or Daddy?'

Johnno raised his bat like he was gonna throw it, but Ben gave him a look.

Shane jumped the net to Ben's end of the court. 'Go on then. We'll play singles til ya get back.'

* * *

Ben checked the toilets first, but there was just a couple of nervous grade ones taking a piss at either end of the urinal. No one was using the cubicles.

He ran down to the edge of the oval, climbed up the fort, and looked across the school. Pokey was out on the oval. He was wrestling with Kevin Hester, an enormous farm boy who was his best friend. Kevin Hester was a Jehovah's Witness. Ben didn't know exactly what that was, but Fab said it meant his family didn't have a telly and were into religious shit. He reckoned they were like the people in that *Witness* movie with Harrison Ford.

Kevin Hester was kind of scary. He had to leave the class when they had religious instruction. So did the Hickey twins, who were Jehovah's as well, but they were both pretty good looking. Ben sometimes wondered what the Hickeys did when they had to leave the class, but was too shy to ask.

Once he'd climbed back down the fort, Fab tapped him on the shoulder.

'Hey, are we still playing bat tennis, or what?' He was puffing like he'd been running.

'Where'd you go?'

'Nowhere. Just getting a drink, like I said.'

'Really?'

'Yeah!' He put his hands on his knees, leaned over for a few seconds and caught his breath. 'C'mon, let's get back. Lunchtime's nearly over and I wanna beat Johnno.'

'I was a bit worried.'

Fab laughed. 'Jesus! Who are ya, my mum? I can look after myself, y'know.' He slapped him on the shoulder. They walked back toward the bat tennis court. 'Did I tell ya I'm goin rabbiting after school?'

'Whereabouts?'

'Dunno. My father's taking me.'

It was the first time Fab had mentioned his dad since the broken window. He looked at Ben, searching for a reaction. Ben met his gaze and forced a smile. 'That's good. Has everything been...'

'Yeah, much better. Maybe you can come around again sometime. Mum said it's okay.'

Ben couldn't imagine anything worse. He'd quietly decided, though he'd never tell Fab, that he never wanted to see Mr Morressi ever again.

'Yeah, maybe,' he said.

* * *

It was the next day that Mr Burke told the class the news.

Kevin Hester wasn't coming to school. Not for a long time. He was in hospital. He'd broken his shoulder.

Burke then launched into a long lecture about bike safety. It seemed like he'd finished, but then he started another boring story of a near miss he had with a truck ten years ago, out on Navarre Road.

But it wasn't til recess that Ben got the proper story from Johnno.

'I saw the whole thing!' His eyes were wide and he bounced from one foot to the other. Ben had never seen him so excited. 'He was riding Pokey's new BMX, right? The Mongoose. The chrome one. Shit-hot bike, right? Pokey let him ride when he asked. I heard him ask. Pokey said no at first, but then Kevin was gonna hit him, right? So we all watched him ride it down the hill. He was flying. Then it happened.'

Ben shook his head. 'What happened?'

'Dontcha know?'

'Nah.'

'Didn't Fab tell ya?'

'Nah.'

'The front wheel came clean off the bike!'

'You're joking.'

'Nah, serious! And Hester just crashed into the road, head first! He was screaming! Blood everywhere. It was just un-be-lievable!'

Ten

The dry heat of summer had begun to ease and the southerly breezes brought relief from the airless nights. Sleep came more easily. Ben would lie awake in the mornings, before his parents woke, the air cool on his skin. His mum had given him an extra blanket and it smelled clean. She said it was a special one, an Onkaparinga with satin trim.

Onkaparinga.

Ben had no idea what it meant, but he liked the sound of the word and the feel of the satin trim on his cheek. He felt safe and warm underneath that blanket and he sometimes wished he could stay there forever.

A month passed before Ronnie wanted him again. He didn't want Ben to mow the lawn this time. He wanted help with his shed.

He rang Ben's mum on the Thursday to organise it for Sunday. Ben heard his mum on the phone, asking why he didn't just drop over instead of wasting money on a phone call.

After she got off the phone, she told Ben's dad that they should invite Ronnie for dinner sometime, seeing he was all on his own like that. Dad didn't say anything. Not right away. He waited til the ads came on. Then he said that he reckoned

Ronnie went out of town a bit, because the car wasn't there much.

'Might have a girlfriend,' he said, 'maybe in Ballarat or somewhere.'

Ben knew he didn't have a girlfriend, but didn't say anything.

* * *

When Ben got there on Sunday, Ronnie wasn't outside. Ben knocked at the front door and part of him hoped Ronnie wouldn't answer. That he'd had a change of plans. That he'd done the job himself.

The ten bucks was good, but the weekends felt too short, especially since Mr Burke definitely hadn't got cancer or AIDS and definitely hadn't died.

He decided to wait for another ten seconds. He counted them under his breath – *four... five... six* – and got faster as he went.

He got to eight when he heard the footsteps inside.

The door swung open.

'G'day mate,' Ronnie said.

He was in his mining gear and he looked out past Ben and into the street. He stepped out to the porch and looked up and down the road, almost like he was expecting someone else, then stepped back inside.

'Jeez, warm again isn't it?' he said.

Ben thought it wasn't really. 'Yeah, I spose.'

Ronnie held the door open and stood to one side, motioning Ben to pass under his arm. 'Come on then.'

He walked past Ronnie and into the lounge room. He'd been in there once before, when Daisy's family still lived there. Joe had invited him over to watch cartoons, but it turned out they were just the Channel Two ones, which were pretty crap: *Danger Mouse*, *The Rocky and Bullwinkle Show* and *Roger Ramjet*. He didn't go round there again after that.

This time it was darker inside and the curtains were closed. The telly was on in the corner, but paused on some close-up he couldn't make out, the static lines slowly cascading down the screen. It looked like someone's leg bent over the edge of a bed, or maybe on a towel. There were empty beer bottles on the coffee table and the smell of smoke was really strong.

'We'll go through to the back.' Ronnie's voice sounded rougher than normal. He brushed past Ben and led the way. Ben followed him down a short passage to the back door. In the passage, both bedroom doors were wide open.

In the first bedroom, there was gym equipment – a bench and dumbbells – set up in front of a big mirror. It was a York bench press set – Ben had seen it in Sportspower and it was expensive. Two hundred and ninety-nine bucks. That first bedroom used to be Daisy and Joe's room. They had to share a bunk.

In the other room, he saw the end of a double bed with a purple blanket crumpled at the bottom. That was Mr and Mrs Wolfe's old room, though he'd never seen inside it before. Clothes were all over the floor – socks, undies and everything. It was a real mess and it kind of stunk as he passed, a bit like Vicks Vaporub, but stronger.

'The work shouldn't take long today, mate.' Ronnie pushed open the back door and Ben noticed how he didn't look at him as much as he normally did, that he kept his eyes down.

* * *

It was nearly four o'clock when he finished loading the boot of Ronnie's car. The shed was filled with bits of timber, corrugated iron and old bottles mostly. Ronnie stayed inside the whole time, he didn't even ask him if he wanted a drink.

When he was done, Ben shut the boot and knocked on the back door.

'Coming!' He heard Ronnie's voice from a long way inside.

Ben walked back across the yard to the shed. He figured if Ronnie saw his work was okay, he'd just pay him the tenner and he'd be able to leave down the driveway. There was no need to go back inside.

Ronnie unlocked the back door, then swung the flyscreen open. 'Sorry, mate, was in the shower.' He came out to the top step. His hair was flat and wet and he wore a red dressing-gown. 'Just did a bit of a workout.' Ben noticed how a thick, blue vein stuck out of his neck when he spoke.

'I'm finished.'

Ronnie walked down the steps and across the yard. He inspected the shed, whistling a bit through his teeth, and then opened the boot of his car. He seemed happier than before and moved quickly, his thongs slapping the cement as he went.

'Nice job, mate.' He leaned with one hand on the shed and turned back to face him. It was then, in the fading sunlight, that Ben realised why his eyes looked weird – one was blue and one was grey. 'Great to get rid of all that old crap.'

He came back to the middle of the yard, placed his right hand on the centre pole of the clothesline, then gently spun the top with his left. His eyes followed its slow revolution. 'Be nice to get rid of this bloody thing too.'

Ben watched it spin and creak.

'Make a bit of room, y'know? Have a barbecue or something. Owner won't let me, but.' He watched it go round just once, then caught it in his hand. 'I asked em. But no chance.' He spun it back the other way. 'Be nice to have a barbecue out here, dontcha reckon? Or maybe one of those tennis things, Toto tennis or whatever it's called. They look like fun, dontcha think? Could have a game, me and you.'

Ben shrugged. It was totem tennis, not toto. 'I spose. Yeah.'

Ronnie smiled as the clothesline creaked to a stop. 'Ya know what happened out here, dontcha?' He reached down and loosened the waistband of his dressing-gown.

Ben scratched his arm. 'Um, I think so.'

Ronnie looked at Ben, laughed a little, and shook his head.

'The silly bitch.'

Ben felt his chest go tight. He didn't like Ronnie calling Daisy that. Maybe he should say something. Ronnie didn't know her, not like he did.

'Ya know why she did it?' Ronnie put both his hands on one of the steel bars of the clothesline and bent his knees, letting it take his full weight. It moaned and heaved to one side.

'Nah.'

Ben heard the squeal of brakes as a car pulled up out front. He looked down the driveway but couldn't see anything. Maybe the Pickerings next door.

Ronnie's gaze flicked over the fence, then back at Ben. He spoke more softly. 'Do you wanna know why?' And he got that funny smile again that stopped in the corner of his mouth.

'I dunno...' Ben wondered if Ronnie might know about the gob jobs too. He slowly stepped toward the driveway. 'But I better—'

'Nah, mate, where you goin?' Ronnie let go of the clothesline and it sprung back up. His funny smile disappeared and he quickly tightened the waistband of his dressing-gown. 'Come inside, mate, and have a drink.' He walked to the steps. 'Gotta pay ya anyway. And I'll fill you in, y'know. About what happened and that.'

'Um, it's getting late and I—'

'C'mon, mate, your mum won't have dinner ready for a while yet. I could use the company.' His lip twitched a little. 'I don't get much company, y'know? I told ya that.'

Ben didn't feel like he could say no, even though he wanted to, pretty much more than anything in the world.

'Okay,' he said.

'Good boy.' Ronnie smiled, properly this time.

Ben looked at the house as he walked up the steps. It was ugly, with its steel windows and cracked, peeling weatherboard. Ben thought about Daisy and how that would have been the last thing she saw. He felt sharp stabs of pain in his chest and his belly.

The silly bitch.

He should've stuck up for her.

* * *

Ronnie moved quickly ahead of Ben in the hallway, almost running, like he forgot something. He called out from the lounge room, 'Wait a sec, just putting the telly on.'

He was fiddling with the remote control and the screen went from loud snow, then to black, then back to life. It was something about the ocean.

'Bloody remote, useless things.' He threw it on the couch. 'Take a seat, mate.'

Ben noticed the beer bottles were all gone.

'Make yourself comfy and I'll get you that drink. You must be thirsty after all that work.'

Ben sat down and decided he would drink whatever Ronnie gave him as quickly as he could. A shark was on the telly, a white pointer. A man was in a cage in scuba gear, watching it swim by.

Ronnie returned from the kitchen with a can of sarsaparilla. Ben hated sars.

'Thanks,' he said.

Ronnie sat down on the edge of the coffee table. Ben cracked open the can and drank. It tasted like old, sweet liquorice. It wasn't that cold, like it had only just gone in the fridge.

'So here's your ten bucks.' Ronnie passed him a ten-dollar note, folded between his fingers. It was one of the new plastic ones. 'Are you saving for something then, or what?'

Ben looked at the note. It had a picture of a ship from the First Fleet. Mr Burke had been talking about it at school, even though in grade five they'd done heaps on it because of the bicentennial. It was all about convicts and shit like that. It was so boring.

'Um, maybe some runners. Nikes.'

Ben pushed the note into his pocket, took another swig of the sars and watched the telly. The shark was gone now and there was an old man with a foreign accent talking about diving for abalone. Ben heard a car drive slowly past outside.

Ronnie didn't say anything for a while, but Ben could tell he wasn't watching the telly. He could feel his eyes on him and hear the slow whistle of air through his nose. He took another deep drink of the sars.

'Nikes, eh? Pretty fancy.'

Ben nodded. He'd almost finished the can. The man on telly was diving underwater for the abalone. He didn't have any scuba gear and Ben wondered if the shark was there somewhere.

'So, the girl who lived here. She was a bit of a hottie, wasn't she?'

Ben shrugged. That shark had to be there somewhere.

'Y'know why she did it?'

Ben kept his eyes on the telly. He'd already told him he didn't. He shook his head.

Abalone.

'Her old man. Her dad.' Ronnie was whispering. 'He was giving her one. Fucking her real regular, y'know?'

Ben's ears went hot, then his face too. The can crunched a little in his hand. The man was back in the cage.

Abalone.

Abalone.

'The boys down the mine told me. She was a real hottie, they said. And he was giving it to her proper. Wasn't the only one, by all reports.'

Ben downed the last of the sars. It was warm and thick on his tongue.

By all reports.

Old men and the sea.

Old men and abalone.

Abalone.

'*A real fuckin hottie*.' Ronnie's breaths had gone all deep and slow. He shifted a bit forward. 'Couldn't blame him, they reckon.' Deep breaths. Deep and slow and rough. 'She was ripe for it. *Ripe for it*. That's what they say.'

Ben's ears throbbed.

'What do you reckon? You musta seen her. Did ya like her? Like her tits?'

Ben shrugged. His whole body was on fire.

Abalone. Old men. Old men and the sea.

His dick was hard in his shorts.

By all reports.

Abalone. Abalone. Abalone.

Nothing could stop it. Not even the shark.

Ronnie laughed. 'I reckon ya did, mate. But it's all right, I'll keep it a secret.' He rustled Ben's hair, softly with his fingers. 'And I'll stop asking questions.'

He brushed Ben's cheek with the back of his hand. His skin felt cool. Cool and smooth.

'Ah! I nearly forgot that other thing I promised ya.'

He reached under the coffee table and pulled out a bunch of magazines, stacked in a pile. He flicked through until he found the one he wanted. 'Mmmm, yeah. Here.'

He held up the cover of the magazine so Ben could see. It had a naked woman and a man on the front, and the title was in another language – German or something. The man had a thick moustache and he was behind her, holding on to her bum with a strange expression on his red, sweaty face, like he was concentrating hard. She had her hands tied to a wooden bench, with her big boobs hanging down like balloons. She looked like she was in pain, her mouth wide open. Ben looked at her boobs and her bum up in the air and his dick started going stiff again.

Ronnie rolled it up and passed it to him. 'Don't tell your mum or anyone, right?'

Ben grabbed hold of the mag. His head swam and he went to drink the sars, but forgot there was none left. His mouth felt dry and sticky. On the telly, the shark was back and was circling the man in the cage.

Ronnie smiled at him. 'Let me know if you like that one.'

Ben nodded.

He couldn't believe what he'd heard. He just couldn't. But he was really looking forward to showing Fab what he'd got.

Eleven

The front door was the best option. Down the hallway, straight into the bedroom.

'Is that you, Ben?'

Mum called out as soon as he came in. *Shit*. She was in the kitchen. Not bad, but backyard or laundry would have been better.

'Yep.' He took a few careful steps down the hallway.

'How did you go?' It sounded like she had an old movie on the black and white telly.

'Good. Just gotta go to the toilet.' The toilet? *Fuck*. He just blurted it out.

'Okay,' she said.

He rushed into the bathroom, which was between his room and his parents', and shut the door behind him. He looked at his face in the mirror. It was bright red. His eyes were glassy.

Daisy. Her dad. Could it be true?

It all seemed like a strange dream, like something he'd imagined. Maybe Ronnie made it up. It was probably just a joke and Ronnie would laugh about it next time. He was just playing a trick on him and he would laugh that he had him fooled.

There was no way – it just couldn't be true. Dads wouldn't do that to their daughters. No way.

He flushed the toilet, ran the tap for a second, then slunk into his room. He wouldn't have long til the movie would be over. Before she'd wanna talk. She always liked to talk, especially when Dad wasn't home.

He hid it behind the wardrobe. There was a gap of a few inches there and it slid down to the floor, out of sight. He sat on his bed, looking at the wardrobe's dark wooden doors, imagining all the possible scenarios.

His mum wanting to shift the furniture around.

His dad looking for something he'd lost.

A sudden spring clean.

No – he had to hide it somewhere else. Somewhere outside. Anywhere inside the house was too risky.

He waited til the telly clicked off. He knew that when the movie ended, his mum would let out a long sigh, turn on the kettle, then go to the toilet.

She always did the same thing. Like clockwork.

* * *

He rolled up the magazine and pushed it down the back of his shorts, right down into his undies, and pulled his t-shirt over the top. He looked in the mirror and it poked through a bit, but at first glance you wouldn't know.

As soon as he heard the toilet seat go down, he walked quickly from his room, through the laundry, and out the back door. The magazine was scratching his arse, so he pulled it out and carried it like a relay baton. His heart beat fast, just having it out in the open air like that, even though no one could see.

Sunny followed him down the back and behind the shed. He wished that Sunny wasn't watching him, even though he was just a dog. It seemed like he could tell something was up, the way he was sniffing around his feet.

Between the fence and the back of the shed there was a

narrow gap about a metre wide. It was where his dad kept a whole lot of old steel and crap that his mum reckoned should go to the tip. No one ever went down there, not even his dad; it was full of red-backs, rust and sharp edges – the perfect spot.

But, before he hid it, he should just have a look. Just a quick one, so he knew what was inside. Just for a minute.

It couldn't hurt.

* * *

Almost every page was full of naked women. Lots of them had dicks in their mouths, sometimes two at a time. The dicks were huge, thick and veiny and the men were all hairy as. Ben thought about his own hairless dick and how small it was compared to those ones. He wondered if it would get bigger. He hoped like anything that it would.

The women mostly had blonde hair, except for a few, but pretty much all of them had huge boobs. There were close-up photos of their fannies. Ben had never seen that before. They had a patch of soft-looking hair and were all pink and fleshy looking.

Some of their fannies looked wet and slippery. Some had big dicks poking inside their fannies. Some had thick, white cum smeared on their faces, their boobs, and in their mouths.

Ben hadn't come before. Fab hadn't either and he reckoned it didn't happen til you were older. Once, they both had a wank at the same time when they went camping, to see if they could come. But it didn't work and they never ever talked about it again. Ben had noticed though that Fab's dick was bigger than his, longer and a bit thicker. It also still had the skin on top, which only a couple of kids at school had, as far as he knew.

Once, when Ben had wanked in the bathroom, a bit of clear liquid had come out, but that was it. He wondered if he might be infertile, but he didn't say anything to Fab. He thought if he wanked harder it might happen, eventually.

He turned the pages and started to feel woozy. His mouth fell open and his breaths became deep. In some of the photos the women had a dick inside their fanny and another in their mouth, their tongue all over it. They all looked like they were right into it. The men looked kind of angry though – with red sweaty faces and serious eyes. Almost like they weren't enjoying it that much.

Ben felt a tingle and his dick was as hard as a rock – he needed a wank something terrible. But it would have to be fast, much faster than his mum could drink a cup of tea. He didn't think that would be a problem.

He looked around but no one could see him there. He held the mag in one hand and pulled down his shorts. His dick looked about a quarter of the size of the ones in the photos, the eye staring back at him all pink and shiny. It didn't have any veins in it, not like the thick ones in the photos. He concentrated on a curly-haired woman with two big dicks in her mouth and started to pull.

Then he heard the back door squeal open.

'Ben!'

His breathing stopped and he was stuck, frozen, holding his dick, with his shorts at his ankles.

Mum.

He could hear her coming up the path.

He couldn't move. This was the end. She'd probably die from a heart attack and he'd be there, paralysed, clutching his dick. Then his dad would kill him and probably go to jail for it.

He tried to roll up the mag but his fingers were shaking and the pages scrunched. He dropped it on the ground and pulled up his shorts, his dick poking through the nylon like a beak.

'Ben! Are you out there?'

Footsteps. Crunching grass. Closer.

'Coming, Mum!' his voice cracked. He picked up the mag, rolled it up as best he could and shoved it in a steel pipe.

He stepped out from behind the shed, but tripped on an old metal box, scraping his knee on a length of old guttering. 'Shit!'

His mum stood a few metres away with her hands on her hips, frowning, with Sunny panting at her feet.

'What are you doing back there?' she said. Then she smiled a bit and Ben wondered why.

'Nothing.'

He stepped slowly toward the house, his body angled away from her view, as he counted backwards through his twelve times tables.

* * *

Ben held on to his secret til Monday lunchtime. Til they were playing two-square in the yard.

Fab's eyes lit up. 'Where'd you get it?'

'I found it.'

'Where?'

'Out the tip.'

Fab whacked the tennis ball into his square. 'Yeah, sure.'

Ben batted back defensively. 'I did!'

Ben's voice went shrill and he knew Fab would know he was lying.

'Bullshit.' Fab smacked the ball into the left corner of Ben's square and it bounced across the asphalt of the netball court, to where some girls sat in a circle. It hit Melissa Hickey in the back and all the girls in the circle turned around.

'Go get it,' Fab said.

'Nah, you go get it. You hit it.' Ben didn't want to run over there with the girls watching him.

'You know the rules, loser fetches.'

Melissa's twin, Jodie, picked up the tennis ball. The Hickeys were definitely Jehovah's, but they were also definitely different to Kevin Hester. They looked normal and dressed normal. Jodie had really big boobs and Fab reckoned he'd seen them after school one time. He'd dared her to flash em and she pulled her t-shirt right up. Ben wasn't sure if it was true, but he liked to believe it was. They were huge, Fab said, and he reckoned he might become a Jehovah too one day.

'All right,' Fab crossed his arms. 'I'll get it, but you gotta tell me where you really got that mag. *And* you gotta show it to me.' Fab was off before Ben could answer. He watched him jog over to the girls. He stood there with his hands on hips, then stuck his hand out for the ball. Jodie threw it but it missed by miles and all the girls laughed at her. Fab ran after it and threw the ball back to Ben.

'You seen Pokey?' Ben said.

Fab's face went a bit tight. 'C'mon, serve.'

'He'll get ya eventually.'

Fab frowned, his eyes dark. 'Just serve, will ya? Bell's gonna go soon.'

Ben tapped the ball into Fab's square. 'He'll work it out, y'know.'

Fab knocked the ball back to Ben's left side. 'I had to try something. I'm sick of him. And it nearly worked, didn't it?'

* * *

It was Friday after school when Ben showed him. They were out the back, behind the shed. Ben didn't feel safe shifting it from there, even though he was starting to think it was a shit spot, that it would probably get wet when it rained.

Fab couldn't believe it.

'Fuuuuck...' he breathed. 'Look at that!' He pointed at a woman getting it from three men.

'Be quiet will ya, I don't want Mum to come out like last time.'

'Fuuuck...' Fab held the mag like it was something fragile, precious.

'Yeah, I know.'

'My cousin Marco has some *Playboys* and that, but nothing like this.' Fab slowly turned the pages. 'Fuuuuck.'

It was hot behind the shed and Ben was shit-scared his mum would find out. Plus, he was worried about spiders.

He reached for the mag. 'C'mon, that's enough I reckon.'

'Just a sec.' Fab pulled away, his eyes as wide as Ben ever saw. 'Whoa, what is this shit?'

Ben only got a glimpse of it. A woman. *A girl*. She was young. A man and a horse. She had her hand on one and her mouth on the other. Ben grabbed the mag off Fab and rolled it up, his hands wet with sweat.

Fab laughed, but it wasn't his normal laugh, more like he forced it. 'There's weird stuff in there,' he said.

'Hadn't seen that bit.' Ben felt his face go hot and he pushed the mag back in the pipe. 'C'mon, let's go.'

Ben turned and climbed back slowly along the fence line, over the scraps of metal and sharp steel.

'Watch ya step,' he said.

'So, who gave it to you?'

'I told ya. I found it.'

'Stop talkin shit.'

'I did!' His voice went shrill again. *Jesus Christ*.

'If you don't tell me, I'll tell Jodie Hickey that you like her.'

Ben stopped and turned around. 'Just get stuffed, will ya?'

'You like her big pillow tits and her Jehovah ways. They've got no telly, so she'll be raring to go. Nothing else to do.'

Ben laughed. 'Rack off.' He kept moving across the steel.

'C'mon, just tell me. I won't tell anyone. Promise.'

'Nah.' Ben shook his head.

'Wait a minute ' Fab stopped. 'I know.'

Ben turned. 'What?'

'It's that guy up the road, isn't it?'

'Who?'

'Ronnie with the Statesman. Your boss.' Fab nodded and smiled like a shit. 'He gave it to ya, didn't he?'

'Nah.'

Fab's smile widened and he crossed his arms. 'Yeah, he did.'

Ben leaned against the fence. 'Okay, yeah. So what? He said he might give me some more too.'

'No shit?'

'Yeah. Don't tell anyone, but.'

'Nah, course not. When are you goin back?'

Ben shrugged. 'Maybe this weekend.' He looked at the ground between the steel and timber, to where a trail of bull ants streamed on an unknown mission. 'He's a bit funny though.'

'What do ya mean?'

'Said some weird things.'

'About what?'

'Um... I dunno. Nothin really. He just looks at me a bit funny.'

'What? You reckon he's a perve or something? Like Jimmy Shine?'

'Dunno. Don't think so. He doesn't look like one.'

Fab smiled. 'Well, whatever happens, just make sure you get one for me.'

'Piss off, will ya?'

Ben turned back and they both climbed carefully over the rusty steel, with its sharp edges, bull ants, and the red-backs sleeping somewhere underneath.

Twelve

Jodie Hickey was in Ben's bed.

She was under the blanket. That nice Onkaparinga with the satin trim that smelled so clean. She had a big smile on her face. It looked like she didn't have a top on. Ben felt so horny. Like he never had before.

She told him to come closer. Fab said something then, because he was in the room too, but then he went away.

Ben went closer.

Then the blanket was gone and she was there, all naked. She was on the bed with her big boobs and white legs.

Soft, pink, slippery.

He mouthed the words.

He went closer.

Jodie smiled and brushed her hair and said there was no need to worry. They could watch telly and have ice-cream after. Vanilla ice-cream.

Vanilla. After Ben was finished.

After Ben...

Ben.

Ben.

'Ben.'

'*Ben!*'

His mum stood at the end of the bed. His dick was so hard it hurt, throbbing against the weight of the blanket. He felt horny and a bit sick all at once.

He turned over and buried his head in the pillow.

'Time to get up!' She reached under the blanket and tickled his feet. 'You'll miss the bus. C'mon!'

* * *

Like Ben had told Fab, Pokey was always gonna work it out. Eventually.

It happened at the bus stop. Not in the morning though. It was the afternoon, out the front of the school. It was Friday. They must have had it all planned out.

Ben had warned him. And he'd been on the lookout himself. But it didn't change anything.

It wasn't Pokey who got him though. Not at first. Jason Kettle, one of Pokey's other friends, got it started. Fab was just standing there. He was looking up the street for the bus. Ben had just said something to him about Burke. And Kettle came with a basketball.

He did it with a run-up. He came in fast and threw the basketball as hard as he could into the side of Fab's head. The ball bounced off it and out onto the road. It rolled all the way over the other side of the street and into someone's front yard. That's how hard he threw it.

Fab didn't even make a noise. He just folded down into the dirt like he was made of nothing. The Hickey twins and some of the other girls screamed. Then Pokey came from the other side.

It was all planned like that. Ben could tell – he could see it all so clearly. Pokey came when Fab was already on the ground. Fab looked like he was dead. Really dead. And Pokey started kicking him. Full kicks. Right in the guts. Like a football. But Fab didn't even move or make a noise.

Like he was really dead for sure.

Thirteen

It was two weeks later, a Friday, when Ronnie rang Ben's mum again. She asked him to come over for a coffee, but he said he was out of town, which was weird because Ben saw the Statesman drive past school that lunchtime. But he didn't say anything.

Ronnie said he didn't have any work for him this weekend, but was going yabbying instead. He wanted to know if Ben could come – a bit of extra reward for his hard work. She told him Ben had hurt his hand playing football, but it should be okay.

At dinnertime, they had fish fingers and mash, which was the same most Fridays. *MacGyver* was on the little telly, but the sound was turned right down. You could still tell what was happening though. *MacGyver* and *The A-Team* were both good like that, you could watch without the sound while you were eating.

Ben waited until his mum had finished her dinner.

'Can I ask Fab to come?'

'Where?' she said.

'Yabbying. With Ronnie.'

His mum took her plate to the sink and rinsed it. 'Don't

see why not.' She got Ben's dad another beer from the fridge. 'What do you reckon?'

His dad shrugged and kept eating his mash.

Ben rang Fab after dinner, but Fab said he was going with his dad to Dimboola for an auction. Farm equipment. But then he rang back straight after to say he could come after all.

* * *

Fab's mum dropped him at Ben's house before breakfast. She beeped the horn and kept the engine running out front. Ben's mum waved to her from the front door.

'She must be in a hurry,' she said. She told Ben to go help, 'Quick.'

Fab's mum drove an old white Valiant Pacer. Ben knew that it was a Valiant because Fab told him. Fab's dad had told him it was a classic and to always be careful in it. Ben thought that if Mr Morressi told you something like that, you'd do exactly what he said.

Ben ran to the footpath. 'Hang on, I'll help you with the nets.'

Fab was reaching deep inside the boot, which was enormous, like a deep black cavern.

'What about your hand?' he said.

'It's okay. I can use it now.' He held it up in front of Fab. He liked the look of his swollen knuckles, how they made his hand look bigger. A bit like a man's hand. Almost like Ronnie's. 'How's your ribs?'

'Only hurts with big breaths. Or if I cough.' He lifted up his singlet and showed Ben the ugly yellow bruise, the size of a dinner plate. 'You know where we're goin?'

'Dunno,' said Ben. 'Should be here soon, but.' Ben grabbed the nets and gently lifted them out, taking most of the weight in his left hand. 'How come you didn't go to Dimboola?'

Fab picked up two tins of dog food, his hessian sack, and then slammed the boot shut. 'He needed extra room in the Kingswood.'

'What's he buying?'

'Dunno. Rabbit traps maybe.'

Just talking about Fab's dad still made Ben feel a bit sick in his guts. And a bit scared too. He walked round to the side of the car and Mrs Morressi wound down her window. She had her hair pulled back in a ponytail. Red lipstick. But she looked different with her hair like that. Younger.

'Ben!' she smiled. 'I haven't seen you in so long! You look like you grow. You come around soon, yes?'

Ben smiled. The warmth rushed up in his chest and filled him to the brim. 'Yes, Mrs Morressi.'

She clicked her tongue and shook her head. 'Eva!' She reached out and touched his arm. 'You call me *Eva*, remember? You look after Fab now. No more accidents with the footballs, okay?' She looked at his hand and frowned. 'You both be more careful, yes?'

The wind gusted and Ben saw two deep-purple marks on her arm, up under the sleeve.

He smiled and promised that he would.

* * *

Ben's mum made them both pancakes in a rectangle pan that Ben liked because he could cut them into squares, like a grid. He gave Sunny half of one of the pancakes, but then Sunny went outside and threw up, so his mum said not to give him any more and to leave him outside. His mum talked to Fab while she was cooking and asked if his parents were planning any holidays. Fab said he didn't know, but that he hoped so. Ben couldn't imagine Mr Morressi would ever go on a holiday anywhere.

The cartoons were on but they weren't that good. They watched *The Archies* and then *Mr. Magoo*. There was an ad on for Sea World and Ben asked his mum if they could go, but she didn't answer. He didn't really want to go to Sea World anyway, he was just trying to show off a bit in front of Fab.

The sun was coming through the yellow glass in the sliding door and onto the telly, which made it hard to see. But it felt like it was going to be warm, which would be good for yabbies. If it was too cool, they wouldn't come out of their burrows, which were like dark little caves in the mud.

Ben was about to change the channel when there was a knock at the front door. Ben said it wasn't him because he came down the side last time. But then he heard Ronnie talking and his mum inviting him in with that voice she sometimes used when guests were around, like she was Princess Diana or something. He came into the lounge and said g'day.

He was wearing a blue singlet this time, like a shearer might wear, and he looked kind of stiff and strange, standing there in the lounge, in his stubbie shorts and with his long, ropey arms. Like he didn't really belong inside.

Ben's mum introduced him to Fab. Fab said hello and Ronnie nodded, but didn't really look at him. He asked if they were ready to go, but he stared at the telly as he said it, even though it was just ads, like he didn't want to look at Ben either. Ben's mum asked him if he wanted a tea or coffee but he said no and kept staring at the telly, kind of like he was annoyed about something.

As they left, and once Fab was out the door, Ben gave his mum a hug goodbye.

He felt kind of glad that Fab was going with him, that it wasn't just him and Ronnie.

* * *

Ben and Fab sat in the back of the Statesman. It was big in there and warm from the sun – it smelled like pine trees and was much cleaner than Ben's parents' car, which always had receipts and old paper bags in the back from the supermarket.

The Statesman had blue velour seats with leather trim and Ben's feet didn't even reach the floor. There were power windows and Fab started making his go up and down until

Ronnie told him to leave it. Even though they were tinted, you could see outside just perfect, and Ben watched his mum wave from the front bedroom window.

The car took off with a low rumble. Ronnie beep-beeped the horn and Ben smiled as the Statesman powered down the road. He looked across at Fab and saw he was playing with something in his hand.

'What's that?'

'Nothin.'

'C'mon.'

'It's nothin.'

'Jeez, you're such a shit.' Ben waited a few seconds then made a snatch with his good hand.

'Stop it!' Fab hissed. Ben saw Ronnie's eyes in the rear-view mirror and moved back into his seat.

Fab whispered, 'Here then.' He opened his hand to reveal a furry, grey animal paw.

'Jesus, what is it?'

'A rabbit's foot.'

Ronnie gunned the car and Ben looked up and saw they were already at the turn-off for the highway.

'Where'd you get it?'

'My father.' Fab looked unsure, like he was wondering if he should be embarrassed or not. It was the same look he'd had when he first brought a salami sandwich to school. 'It's good luck.'

'Can I borrow it?'

'Nah.' Fab closed his hand and put it back in his pocket.

* * *

Ben stared out the window. They were going fast and it looked like they were on the highway to Horsham. Ronnie had barely said a word and Ben didn't know if he should say something.

He sat up a bit so he could see Ronnie's eyes in the rear-view mirror. 'Thanks for taking us, Ronnie.'

'Yeah, thanks,' said Fab.

Ronnie didn't say anything for a few seconds, but looked at Ben in the mirror. Then he said, 'No worries,' and reached for the radio. Ben felt a little relieved as it came on – that song where everything she does is magic.

'Where are we goin?' Fab asked, raising his voice above the music. Fab was better at talking to adults, which usually annoyed Ben a bit. Ronnie didn't look up in the mirror this time, but turned down the radio.

'I've got a block near Glenorchy. Got a dam on it.'

'Ah right.' Fab's voice had deepened a little in the last few weeks. Ben wondered if he was faking it. 'Has this car got extractors?'

Ronnie glanced back over his shoulder. 'Y'know a bit about cars do ya?'

Fab smiled. 'A bit. My father tells me stuff.'

Ronnie clicked the indicator for a turn-off. 'Well, it's got extractors all right. Some people call em headers though.'

Ben felt like a little kid. His dad never talked to him about that sort of stuff. He probably didn't know much about it himself. He knew about trains and timetables, but he never really talked about that either. He never talked much about anything really.

Ben was glad when Fab and Ronnie stopped talking about cars. Ronnie turned the radio back up again and reached into the console, took out a smoke and lit it, before powering down his window.

In the back seat, all Ben could hear was the roar of the wind.

* * *

By the time they got there the sun was high and it was getting hot in the car. They turned off the main road and up a short, steep dirt track that came to a farm gate. Ronnie stopped the car but kept it running. He got out and walked up to the gate.

The radio had gone mostly static, but you could hear voices still, like they had just gone out of range.

Ben watched as Ronnie struggled with a padlock, which was stuck to a thick steel chain threaded through the gate, then hooked around an old fence post. Fab undid his seatbelt, sat up on his knees, and looked out the back window.

'See anything?' Ben said.

'Nah, just farms. Must be outside Glenorchy. No houses or nothin.' Fab sat back down and reached forward between the front seats, pulling open the console.

Ben grabbed his arm, his eyes wide. 'What are you doin'? Are you crazy?'

'Lemme go will ya! Just seein if he's got more of those skin mags.'

Ben pulled him back. 'Stop it! He'll see!' Fab sat back in his seat, just as Ronnie finally got the lock open. He dragged the gate forward with a rusty groan, then walked back to the car.

Ronnie leaned over the open door, one hand on the roof and the other on his hip. He looked at Fab for a while. A long while. Ben wondered if maybe he'd seen him open the console. But he just stood there – his eyes strange in the sunlight, almost like a wild animal, like a wolf. He was just standing there in the sun with his chest heaving in and out, staring at Fab. Then he turned to Ben.

'Do you wanna ride up front, mate?'

'Yep!' Ben shot Fab a smirk and jumped out the back door.

* * *

Ronnie drove the Statesman up the incline and through the gate. The block opened out and it was bigger than Ben imagined. It was empty, apart from one large gum tree a few hundred metres away, off in the far right-hand corner. Up to the left was a small hill, beyond which he reckoned was the dam. The long yellow grass on the hill seemed almost alive, whipped wildly by the wind. Ronnie stopped the car again and got out to close the gate. He locked the chain.

He drove slowly, the car following a worn path through the grass toward the hill. The tall, dry weeds whacked at the sides and brushed underneath. Ben could see less from the front, but the seat was deeper and comfier. He looked across and Ronnie had his seatbelt off and looked like he was concentrating, his eyes squinting in the sunlight. He had a small, green tattoo under his ear that Ben hadn't noticed before, like a blurry star. Ben looked back to Fab, who had moved to the middle seat to get a better view.

The car was starting to get really hot inside, so Ben was glad when Ronnie opened the windows and the smell of earth and grass came rushing in. Ronnie glanced at Ben.

'What happened to your hand, mate?'

Ben looked down at his swollen knuckles. He wanted to tell him what he'd done. That it was almost like in a movie. That Pokey had cried.

Ronnie would be impressed. Definitely. But it was too risky. He might say something to Ben's mum.

'Playing footy at school. Goin for a mark.'

Ronnie looked at his hand. Then he got that funny smile again. 'Is that right?'

Ben looked at his hand once more. 'Yep.'

* * *

Fab saw the dam before Ben, who was busy looking out to the long, dry grass rushing by his window.

'Is that it?' he called out from the back.

'Yep,' Ronnie said.

Ben looked up and saw the small square dam, cut into the corner of the block. It was muddy and it looked deep, with steep banks at the sides. By the fence line, beside the dam, there was an old wooden pen where they must have done mulesing or something. Ben had seen them do it once on Barry

Jack's farm, where they cut the skin off the sheep's bums to stop the blowies.

Inside the pen was a small tin shed with no front, just a wood frame with rusty sheets on the back, top and sides. Ronnie pulled the car up between the pen and the dam and turned off the engine. It hummed and ticked for a few seconds, then fell silent.

'Better than your usual spot?' he said. He levered the hand-brake with a heavy click.

'Which spot?' Ben said.

'That one near the Leviathan. You go there, dontcha?' He paused and looked Ben in the eyes. His face went a bit tight and he blinked a few times quickly. 'Ya mum told me, I think.' He opened the console and got his pack of smokes.

'Yeah, we go there sometimes. Hasn't been that good lately, but.'

Ronnie opened his door and Ben felt the heat rush in. There was the steady hum of farm flies and it stank like sheep shit.

Ben undid his seatbelt and looked back at Fab, who was still in his seat.

'Are you coming?' he said.

But Fab didn't answer. His gaze was off somewhere in the distance, like he was thinking deeply about something.

Fourteen

The road on the way back from Ronnie's block seemed different to Ben, almost like they had taken a different route.

Maybe it was because he was up front this time. It felt rougher and it seemed to twist and turn a lot more.

'Bastard about the weather,' Ronnie said, peering under the fog on the windscreen.

Ben wiped a small circle on the passenger window with the palm of his hand, careful not to leave streaks with his fingers.

'Yeah,' he said.

He looked out to the brown-green blur of trees and farmland.

Not long after they had arrived at the dam, the wind had come in quick, shifting from the west to a cool southerly, pushing the heavy clouds in from over the Grampians. The rain had fallen in big drops and had felt cold, like it came from way up high. They had barely had enough time to bait the nets.

First, they hid under that little shed to see if it might pass. The rain was so loud on the tin that they couldn't hear each other speak. Then it started to leak inside, so Ronnie yelled to get in the car.

They sat in there a while, silently, waiting for it to pass.

But then Ronnie said they better head home before it got too wet, or they might get bogged out there.

Fab sat in the back and didn't say anything. He'd barely said a word since they got there. He just looked out the window, his skinny brown arms crossed and his singlet all wet. Outside, the rain swept in and the tall, thin gums by the roadside swayed back and forth. Ronnie didn't turn the radio on, so there was just the squeak of the wipers, the low engine rumble and steady drone of rain on steel.

As houses appeared at the roadside, first one or two every few kilometres, then more, Ben felt relief that they were getting closer to town. He looked forward to going home to a warm house, getting changed into some dry clothes – maybe his pyjamas – while his mum made him lunch. Maybe baked beans on toast. Or, if he was lucky, alphabet soup.

'Where's your place, Fab?' Ronnie said, glancing up at the rear-view mirror.

Fab shifted forward in his seat. 'That's okay, you can just drop me back at Ben's.'

Ronnie shook his head. 'Nah, I'll take you home, mate. Don't want you having to walk in the rain.'

Fab nodded and moved back in his seat. 'Seaby Street,' he said.

Ben would have liked it if Fab came over. If the rain cleared, they could play cricket out back. There wasn't as much room as at Fab's, but it was still pretty good. Otherwise, they could stay inside and play Test Match. He wanted to say something, but it just seemed easier to go along with Ronnie.

Ronnie glanced at Ben. 'So, what really happened to your hand, mate?'

His face went hot. He watched the wipers screech left and right. Left and right. 'The footy. It was pretty waterlogged and it hit the end of my fingers. Hurt like hell.'

Ronnie laughed. 'C'mon, mate, you can tell me. I won't dob. Did ya have a punch-on?'

He tried not to smile. 'Yeah.'

Ronnie raised his eyebrows. 'They must have come off second best, by the look. Someone giving you grief?'

Ben hoped Fab couldn't hear from the back. With the rain and everything. 'Yeah,' he said.

Ronnie glanced at the rear-view mirror, then reached over and rubbed Ben's shoulder. 'Well, if they give you any more trouble, you tell me, all right? I'll put a stop to it.' He smiled. 'I'm good at things like that.'

As they turned into Seaby Street, Fab popped his seatbelt and leaned forward, his hand on the console, balancing his weight between the front seats. Ben saw he had the rabbit's foot in his fingers, its grey fur flattened like he'd been holding it tight.

'Wanna come over to my place, then?' he said. 'Mum can drop you off later.' His breath was hot on Ben's neck. 'And he won't be there. My father, I mean. He's in Dimboola til tomorrow.'

But Ronnie jumped in before Ben got a chance to answer.

'Nah, I better take Ben home, mate. Don't want to get in trouble with his mum, do we? Last thing we need. Plus, I've got his gear in the back.'

Fab answered quick, like he'd already thought it through. 'If you leave his stuff at my place, my mum can drop it off later.'

It was a good idea. And it'd be nice to see Fab's mum again, especially without his dad there.

Ben turned to Ronnie, 'Yeah, I think I'll do that... if that's okay, I mean. I can ring my mum from Fab's and—'

Ronnie slapped the steering wheel and looked back at Fab, his face all twisted like Ben had never seen.

'Listen, you little shit! What did I say? I said I'm fucking dropping him home, all right?'

He swung the Statesman hard into the curb, the tyres screeching and launching Fab forward between the seats.

Fab coughed and pulled himself back into his seat. 'Okay,'

he said, his voice shaking. Ben could see his lip quiver, but he tried to hide it, turning away.

Ronnie turned the engine off, took a few long, deep breaths in and out. He rubbed his face with both hands, like he was upset, then turned back to Fab.

'Look, I'm sorry, mate,' he shook his head. 'Get a bit of a temper sometimes. A bit disappointed about the weather, y'know. You right?'

'Yep.' Fab opened the door and got out, even though his house was a lot further up the street. He waited outside on the nature strip and, even with the rain coming down, Ben could see tears in his eyes.

He powered down the window a bit and called out, 'I'll ring ya tomorrow, okay?'

Fab frowned like he hadn't heard him properly. 'What?'

'I'll ring ya!'

Fab shook his head like he still hadn't heard.

Ronnie moved quickly round the back and scraped Fab's nets out of the boot. He didn't even look at Fab or say anything to him, as far as Ben could tell. He just threw the nets and the hessian sack on the nature strip, rubbed his hands together, and got back in the car.

* * *

As he started the engine, Ronnie was smiling. Not his full smile, just a little at the corners of his mouth, but different this time. Like he was trying to hold it in.

'Now,' he said, 'Do you wanna go for a bit of a drive, or back to my place for a bit?'

'Um...' Ben shifted back in his seat. He was scared that Ronnie might get angry again. 'Weren't you gonna drop me off?'

Ronnie eased the car from the curb and accelerated down the street. Ben looked in his side mirror and he could see Fab still standing at the side of the road, in the rain, watching the car.

Ronnie lit a cigarette and opened his window. 'Your mum won't be expecting you for a bit. Thought we might make the most of it, you and me.' Ben noticed he had another tattoo, a small one, on his wrist.

'Um, okay.'

'I've got an old shack in the Black Ranges. Need to pick up a couple of tools out there. Thought maybe you could give me a hand.'

Part Two

One

For a moment, on the burning bitumen of the car park, Fab was transported back fourteen years to his year nine biology class. Like his job, that double-period did not exist in normal space and time.

A large white wall-clock at the front of the classroom marked the pace. Fab remembered that clock more than anything he was taught – the shape of the numbers and its long, red second hand that didn't tick, but spun slowly around on its way to nowhere. His eyes were drawn to the clock's round, stubborn face and its endless, cosmic cycle as Mrs Cooney droned on and on.

'Eh Fab, you workin?' Afriki smiled and crunched another trolley back into the bay. It sometimes seemed like the only English he knew.

'Yes, mate, I'm workin.'

A few months back the local council had got some Sudanese refugees to settle. There was a big deal about it – even a council reception and pictures in the paper. Then they're stuck doing jobs like this.

You can't miss em on a Sunday though, walking up the Main Street to church – seven-foot tall in white polyester suits, their wives in dresses of greens, blues and gold like no one has ever seen.

* * *

At knock off, Fab needed a beer. Afriki was still busy linking the trolleys. A fluoro safety vest draped his narrow frame like an overcoat, hanging to the knees of op-shop slacks a couple of inches too short.

'Hey Afriki, you drinky or what?' Fab did the 'drinky-drinky' gesture, then immediately felt like a tool.

Afriki looked at him with those large, startled eyes, smiled shyly and shook his head, before turning his gaze back to the trolleys.

Stawell had just one decent pub: the Criterion, right over the road from Safeway. Bob Schmidt owned it and had decked it out in a nautical theme. The town was, after all, only 181 kilometres from the sea. The centrepiece was an old timber rowboat that had been converted into seating for four. No one ever sat there. Beside the boat was the Elvira pinball machine where Fab had wasted his high school years, and a few years since.

He pushed through the swinging doors to the main bar. Even with the anti-smoking laws, the place still stank of durries. As usual, in the afternoon, it was empty and silent but for the static anticipation of the bug zapper.

'Here's a familiar face!'

Lucy Schmidt emerged from the kitchen. Bob had recently installed a video camera in the bar so Lucy could still serve customers while she prepared food for the dinner shift. Bob spent all his afternoons asleep in the lounge room upstairs on an inflatable lilo. He reckoned it was better for his back. But everyone knew there was nothing wrong with Bob's back.

'G'day Lucy.'

Fab pulled himself onto his stool at the end of the bar, beside Elvira. He watched Lucy's hips as she came in behind the bar; the blue denim hugged her flesh firmly, but not too tight. He wondered if she had knickers on. He decided that she didn't.

'Usual?'

Fab wished she wouldn't say that. He was keenly aware that his stool used to be Arthur Carter's. Arty had worn a groove in the laminate with his elbow; his tall, thin frame forever tilted against the bar, white hair slicked back above a face like a John Brack painting – all angles and black eyes. When his health got bad the local doctor scared him on to orange juice, so he smoked an extra pack each day to calm his nerves.

'Another day then, eh?'

Fab shrugged. 'Where's all your customers?'

Lucy raised an eyebrow. 'Where's all your mates?'

'Touché.'

She trotted across the tiled bar floor and eased the fridge open with economy of movement. The heavy steel door swung silently on its hinge, revealing the misted bottles and the reassuring whirr of the cooler within.

Lucy still had her apron on and Fab sometimes wondered if she slept in it. As she turned, he watched her round arse in those blue jeans and imagined how it might look naked, but with the apron still tied round the back.

Lucy was from up north, Cairns to be exact. When she talked about the place, it sounded exotic. Fab loved hearing about the palm trees, warm sea water and tropical fruit. He wondered why anyone would leave.

It was about five years earlier that she'd arrived, just passing through on her way to Melbourne. But she never made it that far, not even once.

She swung back across the bar and placed the stubby unopened in front of Fab. She glanced back over her shoulder toward the kitchen and then leaned in close. She smelled like trees. Fresh. Like the honeysuckle down by the river.

'I thought you had that Centrelink appointment?' she said.

He shrugged. 'Tomorrow.'

'Fingers crossed then.' She traced a finger along his arm, tiny goose bumps tingling his skin.

Fab eyed the camera, angled strategically across the bar. 'Where's Bob?'

She arched an eyebrow. 'Where do you think?'

He nodded to the camera. 'Never far away, though.'

'Making you nervous?' she said.

'A little.'

She squeezed his wrist and took his fingers in one hand, her skin like milk against his battered, callused paw. She opened out his hand and traced her fingertips along the deep ravines of his palm.

'Wanna know something?' she said.

'What?'

'Someone asking about you earlier.'

'Here?'

'Yeah.'

'Who?'

The swinging doors suddenly creaked open. Lucy let go of his hand and quickly retreated to the fridge.

Fab cracked the top off his beer and swung around on his stool as casually as he could manage.

'You've knocked off early,' he said flatly.

It was Bernie Stark – one of the meatheads from the abattoir. 'Had to see my darlin Lucy.' He grinned and slapped Fab on the back. 'Looks like this dickhead beat me to it!'

Fab gave him a look.

Lucy fetched a pot from the glass chiller and started to pour. The skin on her neck had flushed deep red.

'Hold on, darlin. I know you like to please old Bernie. But I gotta unleash the beast.' He laughed. 'Back in a tick.'

Fab waited til he heard the toilet door squeal shut.

'Jesus, I hate that prick.'

Lucy shook her head. 'He's not the worst.'

'Anyway, you were saying? Someone asking about me?'

She left the pot at the taps and came in close. 'Yeah, soon after we opened.'

Fab took a sip of his beer.

'A suit. Reckoned he knew you worked over the road.'

Fab's mind raced. 'What did he wanna know?'

She shrugged. 'Just general stuff.'

'What did ya say?'

'Said you kept to yourself.'

The toilet door squealed open and Bernie let out a long burp. 'Jesus! That's better.'

Fab leaned back on his stool and sucked at his beer. He mentally recounted the list of people he might have pissed off in the past few months – maybe four or five?

No one he couldn't deal with.

Two

He had it figured. It was after the second cone that the idea came to him. By the fourth it was a dead-set certainty. The man in the suit was a private investigator. Hired by WorkCover.

Fab used to work at the abattoir, boning beef. By Friday of his first week, he was almost getting the hang of it.

He was working his way through the last carcass of his shift. It was hard going, physical, and you had to use your hands and angle the blade just right, get it between the joints, through the sinew and tendons. You had to be precise. He was almost starting to enjoy it.

And that's when they got him.

Four of them.

They grabbed him from behind, slung him down and carried him off. Bernie Stark was the ringleader.

'You're gonna cop it now. Initiation!'

He put up a fight at first, but it was no use. He remembered their faces, ugly grins and blue shower caps, coming in and out of sight as they swung him from side to side.

One! ... Two! ... Three!

He was airborne for just a second, then underwater.

But it didn't feel like water.

It was thick like cold soup and there were things in there.

Soft things. Harder things. Strange shapes.

His feet found the floor – he stood up and opened his eyes, but they were covered in muck. The taste in his mouth, like raw meat on the turn.

And all he could hear was their laughter.

They'd thrown him in the guts pit, a putrid pool of thick blood, snaking intestines and fat jelly livers. He was covered head to toe in blood and shit. He was like Carrie at the prom. Except Bernie Stark wasn't John Travolta. And Fab didn't have special powers.

The smell stayed on his skin for days. He could never look at meat pies again after that. Just the thought was too much. And he couldn't go back to work at the abattoir either.

That's where the WorkCover claim came in – psychological injury. It was mostly the doctor's idea. Regular certificates and monthly payments – a sweet deal.

But after a while the money wasn't enough. Especially with all that spare time on his hands. And especially when the local dope got more expensive.

Pushing trolleys had been perfect til now – paid in cash and not much thinking to it. Spending money. Recreation.

The trolley job was Plan A. It was the right time for Plan B.

* * *

Fab wore his only clean t-shirt for the Centrelink appointment. It had a Campbell's soup tin on the front. He didn't really get Warhol. The only thing Fab knew about him was his real name. Warhola. He saw it on a documentary once.

The Centrelink office was in Ballarat, a two-hour bus ride from Stawell. The queue was grinding Fab down. Some French students were in front trying to get Austudy. The receptionist unleashed her best bureaucratese. They had no chance.

Next in line was a middle-aged junkie. He had a full-body twitch, dragging his right hand down his left arm, kicking out his left leg and jerking his head backwards. He was making people nervous and Fab wondered what he was there for. Career counselling? Training? Wasn't addiction a full-time job?

The French girls walked out confused. They should have stayed in France. In the movies, the women there were so beautiful. All milky skin and big dark eyes you could disappear in forever. Like in that movie, *Amelie*.

'Next please.'

He stepped up with a slight frown and thin smile – his practised look of sincerity.

'Yes?'

'I have an appointment.'

'Yes, take a seat over there.' She nodded toward another waiting area. 'They'll call you.'

'For fuck's sake.'

'What was that?'

'Nothing.'

* * *

There were twelve by ten rows of seats, almost all of them taken. Fab stepped over legs and handbags and planted himself next to an Italian signora. Clickety-clack. Knitting something black.

The guy in front had his thick hair slicked back old-fashioned, arm dangling across the chair like a regular, flicking sideways glances at passing ladies. Strong aftershave. Flammable. Chemist brand.

Two girls on Fab's right talked fast with the easy way of long-time friends – one was a skinny-looking country type with a blonde ponytail and a hippie-student look. Denim flares. The other, who Fab could only see out of the corner of his eye, had brown hair and freckles. She sounded heavier, husky.

'How long are you going back for?' said Blonde Girl.

'Just two nights,' said Brunette.

'Why?'

'I have to see my uncle. It's his birthday.'

'How boring.'

'I know.'

'Is it the hot one?'

'Who?'

'The hot uncle.'

'You're so gross.'

'He is definitely hot.'

'Shut up.'

'You know who I mean.'

'I said, *shut up*.'

'It's only incest if you tell.'

It was rapid, soft and continuous, almost intuitive. Fab could only hear it if he concentrated. It was like breath.

'Oh god, what is this?' said Blonde.

Fab looked up at the big plasma TV screen. It was one of the morning shows – the guy from *The Price is Right* and a very excited woman. They were talking vacuums and bowling balls.

Another indignity for the undignified, Fab mused to himself, impressed by his own eloquence.

'*But coming up right now, something special for the ladies... Manpower!*'

'Jesus. It's like these shows are made by someone with ADD,' said Brunette.

'*Laydees, here they come!*'

A dozen steroid types in cowboy outfits rolled out to 'Achy Breaky Heart'. Why was it always cowboy outfits? Did women want to fuck cowboys? Be poked by a cowpoke? He didn't think Lucy would be into that sort of stuff. Not one bit. Even if she was from Queensland.

'Oh... My... God. This is so bad!' said Blonde.

'They are so out of sync. Are they supposed to be out of sync?'

'What's that song?'

'It's so awful.'

'They just look aggro.'

'Hot bodies though.'

'Hmmm.'

'What?'

'Reminds me of someone.'

'Stop it.'

'You know it.'

Fab worked out the cowboy thing – the pants came off easy. But it wasn't dancing – just stomping and thrusting fists.

Fab didn't know where to look. The Italian signora concentrated on her knitting. Aftershave man stared with hard eyes out the window.

* * *

'You should really think about retraining, something to help you get back to work.'

The bureaucrat, with his short-sleeved shirt and long yellow tie, reckoned that selling second-hand stuff on eBay wasn't a business. And it definitely wasn't eligible for a grant.

'We can offer you some counselling to help you overcome...' he paused, as if searching for the right words, '...*the incident*.'

Fab listened, but was distracted by the shininess of the man's oily scalp. He could imagine his head as a smooth white skull, balanced delicately on top of an empty short-sleeved shirt.

And he imagined the floor suddenly opening up to reveal a gaping wound in the earth, and them both sinking slowly down into hell.

* * *

Out in the car park, Fab scanned the surrounds for any sign of the private investigator. He wouldn't be wearing a suit all the time, so he tried to spot anyone looking *too* casual. Aside from a skateboarder, all clear. He walked to the bus stop. His phone rang. Private number.

'Hello?'

'Is this Fab?'

'Yeah.' He tried to place the voice.

'It's Derek.'

'Right...'

'I bought that lamp on eBay off you?'

Shit. Another unhappy customer of DaftJunk77. Fab had underquoted the postage (again) and it was going to cost him more to send the lamp than he was making from the sale.

'You got my message?'

'Yeah, I got your message.' Derek paused. 'I'm not very happy.'

It was easy to type a lie, but harder to say one. Fab took a deep breath.

'Look, I'm sorry. It smashed when I was trying to pack it. Just went right out of my hands.'

Fab caught his own reflection in the window of the Centrelink office, holding the phone hard against his face, his eyes wide and dark hair wild – he looked completely nuts.

'Yeah? Well, I'd like to see some proof that it broke. A photo or something.'

'A photo?' He hadn't planned for that. Shit.

'Yeah. How do I know you didn't just sell it to someone else? Look, I don't want to leave negative feedback, but...'

* * *

That night, Fab locked himself in the shed and prepared to smash his mum's retro lamp into a hundred pieces with a claw hammer. He needed a drink.

He swung down quickly and the glass imploded with a high-pitched, gassy hum.

'What was *that*?' his mum yelled out from the kitchen.

'Nothing!' he yelled.

Three

It wasn't Fab's house. It used to be Sid's place and, in Fab's mind, it always would be.

Sid had worked with Fab's father at the timber mill and would come round to their house sometimes. Fab was scared of him. He was old, drank a lot and spat when he spoke. Mostly his father would go round to his place. He'd be gone for hours and come home reeking of whisky.

At first, Fab's mum had blamed Sid for all the trouble.

Sid was a bit weird. 'How's the young fella?' he'd ask, his breath worse than a dog's. He lived in a run-down weatherboard near the industrial estate, not far from the mill and right over the road from the cemetery. After Sid died, Fab's father bought the house for six hundred bucks and said he paid too much.

After Sid died, there was no one else to blame for all the trouble.

His father didn't buy the land, just the house. He put it on the back of a truck and took it to the block in Stawell West, near the highway.

It was exactly one year later, and the day after Fab's eighteenth birthday, that his father died. A lot of things happened that year. His father dying wasn't the worst. Not by a long shot.

Mum had to sell the family home to pay his father's debts. So they moved to Sid's old place on the block, perched up on timber posts like the house in *The Amityville Horror*.

The heat in summer was unrelenting. The whole block seemed to bake and split as the earth opened up, releasing tribes of angry bull ants and brown snakes. The trees stifled any southerly change and the house would stay hot overnight, with no relief before the next assault of blazing sun.

There was only one door to the outside; Fab had sheeted up the back door with corrugated iron. There were no steps out back and he was worried his mum might forget one day. The wind from the north rattled that piece of iron like crazy. He'd tried to fix it a few times but it always, somehow, shook itself loose.

In the space underneath the house was all his father's old junk. He'd bought a lot of stuff at farm foreclosure auctions, loaded it on the trailer and taken it out to Stawell West.

No one knew why he wanted all that crap, but Fab reckoned he could make some money out of it now.

Farm equipment.

Rustic furniture.

Old iron tools.

People loved that shit, especially city people. Lucy thought it could be a winner too. But the Centrelink man with the shiny head knew fuck-all about that.

Fab had only brought a girl back to the house once. Charlotte Saint-Rose. That was her actual, real surname, Saint-Rose – like a romance novel. But there was nothing saintly or romantic about Charlotte.

She was related to the Ricketts – they were her cousins. The Ricketts were in-breds – a brother and sister who lived together up in the Black Ranges. They had two boys together, twins. No one really knew their names, but everyone called those two boys the lumpy brothers.

Fab had seen them once in the waiting room at the doctors. They both had hats on, but he could still see the lumps on their foreheads. He was one of the only people in town to have ever seen them. They were almost mythical, those twins, like a local version of the Loch Ness monster. Most people didn't even think they were real.

Some people called Charlotte the lumpy sister. Or, less often, but more accurately, the lumpy cousin. But, to be fair, she didn't have any lumps like they did. Or none that you could see, at least.

She was solid, powerfully built – strong legs, big arse and enormous tits. A sure thing. Not that smart, but mad for it. Not much to look at either, not in the face, anyway. She was the type you only ever did on the quiet, especially in a town like Stawell.

Even though it was only Charlotte Saint-Rose, he was embarrassed about his bedroom with its cracked plaster and moist smell, so he'd planned to only get her there when things were ready to go. So he could keep the light off.

The lounge room, with its high ceiling was the best room. They started pashing on the couch and, before he knew it, she got his pants down and was going for it, with the light on and everything. He'd never had a hand job like it. If there was an Olympic sport for it, she'd be a household name. She'd be on your box of Weet-Bix – TV commercials, sponsorship deals – the works. She was like a ninja, the tension and speed just perfect.

And she was about to go down when it happened – his mum came out of her bedroom.

He would never understand why, maybe it was shock or some kind of flight or fight response, but as soon as he saw his mum, bleary eyed and in her dressing gown, he shot his load. He hadn't even been close til then, but it went all over Charlotte's arm and on the couch as well.

His mum looked at him blankly and then went back into her bedroom without saying a word. She never said a thing about it. And Charlotte just kept tugging at him the whole way through, like nothing had happened. She really was so professional about the whole thing.

After that, any time he had a wank, he would fight hard not to think of Charlotte and – more disturbingly – his mum. They always appeared, completely uninvited, even if only for a split second.

The worst was the dream where his mum's face was on Charlotte's body, but that only happened once. He'd been majorly stoned that night and eaten nearly a whole block of Coon.

Apart from Charlotte, most of the girls in town just weren't his type. And, more to the point, he wasn't theirs. But as soon as Lucy started at the pub – that first day he saw her – he knew something was different.

He didn't try to rationalise it. He couldn't.

She'd picked up the job just for extra cash while passing through. Within six months, she'd shacked up with Bob and had been in the kitchen or the bar ever since. Bob had promised that once they were married, she'd never have to work again. But apart from their wedding day, a grand affair at the footy clubrooms, it seemed like she'd barely left the building. Or taken off that apron.

She was a fair bit older, thirty-six, but that didn't bother Fab so much. And they'd never done anything. Not yet. Nothing serious anyway.

There was just the one time, in the pantry out by the kitchen. Saturday night. Bob was asleep upstairs. Just a few seconds. Hot breath. Nervous hands. Slow down, she said. Fumbling, trembling fingers. *Slow down*. Tight jeans and smooth, cool skin. Just a few seconds.

And it was enough. Up until now, at least.

But he had plans for him and Lucy. He just had to play the long game. It couldn't be rushed.

The first step was to sell his father's junk, then fix up the house a bit. Mum might agree to sell it and they could move somewhere else. Ballarat. A change. It wasn't like they had friends in town anyway. They could start afresh. He could get a job at the goldmine up there. Make some real money.

Then Lucy could leave Bob and come live with them for a bit. And once he made enough cash, they could move up north. Somewhere tropical. Mum could come up too, if she wanted.

He had it all worked out, more or less.

Four

Dion Shea was the same age as Fab, but had recently risen to the dizzying heights of Assistant Manager of Safeway.

This meant he got a little name badge and his picture on that special board inside the supermarket. The 'wall of shame', as Fab called it.

Dion appeared to model himself on Shane Warne, with gelled peroxide hair, cheap jewellery, and a mindless habit of adjusting his balls. While he had battled body odour and severe acne throughout high school, Dion now saw himself, somewhat optimistically, as a viable prospect for a quick, no-strings root on a Saturday night. He had the general air of a man who viewed this as a pretty decent achievement in life.

To highlight his success, he'd recently invested in a Celtic tattoo, an eyebrow piercing and a yellow Mitsubishi Lancer with every imaginable aftermarket enhancement. The car was, aside from his own appearance, the number one priority of his world.

'Hurry up, Fab. The shoppers need trolleys, ya know.'

Fab nodded. He sometimes thought Dion might have missed his calling. Motivational speaker.

He'd had just enough time to gulp down a large iced coffee

he'd nicked from the cold store before his shift. He needed caffeine. The job took a lot more effort than most people, even Dion, imagined.

He linked eight trolleys in a long snake and pushed up the hill, dodging people and cars on the way. Daft Punk in his headphones.

He felt someone grab his arm.

He turned, irritated.

A man, late forties. Big eyes and short grey hair. Meaty face. Unsmiling.

In Stawell, Fab knew pretty much everyone. Not this guy. He wore a neatly pressed shirt, which was unusual. He was out of breath.

Fab took his headphones out. 'Yeah, what?'

He tried to look blasé as he studied the man's face for any signs. Signs of someone serious. Someone official. Someone who might want to ask questions.

'You dropped this,' the man said.

Fab looked down at the man's hand – he was holding the rabbit's foot.

Fuck. How had he dropped that?

'I chase you from inside.' The man had a thick accent and he clouted out each word. Maybe German. A tourist.

'Thanks.' Fab took the dried foot from the man's hand and quickly looped the silver chain through his key ring.

'No problem.' The German smiled. 'They say they are good luck, yes?' His head bobbed up and down.

'If you say so. Thanks again.'

Fab pushed the key ring back inside his pocket. He continued toward the trolley bay, where Afriki was trying to fix a busted baby chair with the studied intensity of a brain surgeon. He stopped fiddling with the buckles of the seat and stared at Fab.

'My friend, you look like a ghost.'

'Like I've *seen* a ghost, you mean.' Fab started linking the trolleys.

Afriki nodded, and Fab could see him store yet another strange saying to memory. He never got it wrong twice.

'What happened?' he said.

'Nothing, just lost something. Hey, listen. Do me a favour will ya?'

Afriki frowned and nodded as though he understood, which Fab knew was his way of buying time. He rephrased.

'Afriki, I need you to do something for me.'

'Yes, Fab, of course.' His eyes widened. 'Anything!'

'If anyone comes asking for me, or acting funny, you tell me, okay?'

'Of course, yes.' The frown returned. 'But at my home, when people look for you, is never good thing. Who looks for you, Fab?'

'No one. I mean, maybe someone. Well, I don't know. Just tell me if you notice anyone, okay?'

'Okay, yes.' Afriki smiled and nodded.

Fab pulled the row of trolleys out, put his headphones back in, and pushed back up the hill.

Five

When Lucy picked up the empty, his third stubby in fifteen minutes, she paused before getting the next.

She frowned. 'You all right?' 'Yeah, why?'

'Knocking them back pretty quick. Doing old Arty proud. He'd be pleased you got his seat.'

'I ah... just had a tough day. So listen, has that fella in the suit been around again?'

Lucy leaned forward, placing her elbows on the bar and her hands on her cheeks. 'Jesus, are you getting paranoid or what?' She winked and his heart raced. 'Not today, but you'll be the first to know.'

'Just thinking though, you said he was asking general stuff. Like what?'

She leaned back and crossed her arms. 'Jesus, I dunno. What days you worked, stuff like that. Like I said, I didn't tell him anything.'

She picked up a cloth and wiped down the bar. Fab could tell by the edge in her voice that he should drop it. He tilted the empty toward her.

'Well, you did okay if he hasn't come back.' He forced a smile. 'Better get me one last beer, to celebrate.'

* * *

Three beers later, he stared for a moment at Lucy, just so perfect in her black apron.

She had that low-cut white cotton t-shirt underneath. His favourite, nice and simple. Fab imagined her breasts would be heavy, fleshy – but not too soft. The skin there cool and smooth to touch. He could see a faint blue vein running down her left breast and it made him a bit crazy.

'Kitchen's closing soon, Fab. Nothing to eat? I've got some shepherd's pie if you want?'

'Nah, no pies!' He swayed to the left, but kept his feet rooted to the carpet, eyes fixed on her chest. 'Don't like pies, remember?'

'Steak sandwich?'

'Not tonight.' He slurred and shook his head. 'No room!' He smiled, held up his beer and swayed to the right, just to even things out.

Bernie Stark walked to the bar and reached for a bag of chips. 'Jesus, Morressi. Really falling apart, aren't ya?'

Fab glared.

'Why don't ya come back out to the abs for another swimming lesson?' Bernie dropped a handful of coins on the bar. 'I should be careful though, eh? Me brother told me years ago that you were the Karate Kid!'

Fab put his stubby down on the bar. 'And how is Pokey? Prison treating him well?'

Bernie's face twisted. 'He'll be out soon enough. And you'll get what's coming.'

As Bernie headed back to his table, Lucy placed a hand gently on Fab's wrist. 'C'mon. Don't start any trouble.'

He took a swig of his beer. The dregs were warm and bitter.

'What is it with you two, anyway?' she said.

'It's his brother.' 'Pokey?'

'Yeah.'

'What about him?'

'Same year as me.'

'In school?'

'Yeah.'

'That's a long time ago.'

'I haven't forgotten.'

'Give you a hard time?'

Fab shrugged. 'Something like that. Was pretty shit all round.' He picked at the label of his stubby.

'School?'

'Yeah.'

'Didn't you have any friends?'

He stopped scratching at the label, looked at her, then went back to the task. 'Just one,' he said.

'Only one? Do I know him?'

Fab hesitated. He took a deep breath in and out. 'He's long gone.'

'Keep in contact?'

He shook his head. 'No chance of that.'

'Did he move town?'

Fab handed her the empty stubby, now picked clean. 'Something like that.'

'You should get back in touch.' She smiled. 'Might be nice after all this time, don't ya think?'

He frowned. 'Not that simple.'

'Well,' she squeezed his hand, 'you've got me now at least.'

* * *

After his mum had gone to bed, Fab stumbled out to the front step with a thick joint. Last year, he'd learnt that the bong was no good for outdoors – he'd started a small grass fire when the wind had picked up. He knew a joint was a waste of dope, but he felt a deep need to be outside.

He looked up at the black sky and lit up.

Gradually, it did its work and that rich, sweet warmth flowed through him. He felt light in his limbs and a smile came to his lips as he reached into his pocket for the rabbit's foot.

Fuck, it was lucky that German tourist had a sharp eye. Germans – always so efficient, they never miss a trick.

He pulled it out and felt its fur under his fingertips. He held it up in the darkness – a tatty, dried artefact of his childhood. The only thing his father ever gave him.

He took a long drag and remembered how, in the winter, he and his father would go hunting.

* * *

His father had a special rifle. It lived in his parents' room, which was always open, except late at night when Fab heard the click of the lock, as he lay under his blankets with a hot brick at his feet.

Sometimes he would go in there, while his father was at work. He would go there to look at it – a Beretta, shipped by special order, sheathed in its long leather case that smelled of olive oil – sleeping in the shadows and silk of the dresses his mother never wore. He would carefully unbutton the leather and feel dizzy as the carved yellow maple and black steel emerged from the gloom. He would run his hand along the smooth cold steel of the barrel down to the maple, gently tracing its intricate patterns with his fingertips.

They hunted at dusk in the Black Ranges. The gun always rode in the back of the Kingswood, quietly menacing on the yellow vinyl seat. They would park before the gate and walk from there, but first his father would get the rifle ready. He would open the back door and crawl into the back seat, gently kneeling astride the leather case, unbuttoning from the top first and working slowly down the barrel, the forestock, the butt. He always left the case open on the seat, with its soft interior waiting patiently for its return.

Winter came with a squall from the south, rising over the Grampians and tearing across the flat Mallee farmland. The wind was low and cold and Fab enjoyed the warmth beneath his singlet, shirt, jumper and jacket, hands pushed deep in his pockets. His father would stride ahead in his long woollen coat, rifle slung off one big shoulder and swaying at his side. Fab would squint and imagine they were soldiers, comrades, stalking the dark hills where their enemies lay, waiting and watching.

Fab remembered the first time he saw his father shoot a rabbit. It was in a deep, swampy valley over the third hill. A lone crow called to them from an old gum as they climbed through a wire fence at the valley edge. The way down looked rocky and steep and Fab was scared, worried that the night would fall quickly. As they began to descend in that half-light, all went quiet but the wind; even the crow ended his call, folded his wings and tucked his black beak into his breast.

His father pointed to the bottom of the valley.

'A lot of tunnels,' he whispered, 'full of rabbits.' The air was colder and a mist fell from the range. His father walked slowly and crouched lower, careful to keep hidden from sight. He moved in a gentle arc, upwind of the scent, with the gun held tightly at his side.

He paused and held one hand back, motioning for Fab to stop. Silently, he moved down on one knee, lifted the rifle in both hands, and balanced the stock carefully against his shoulder. Fab could see what he was aiming for: three rabbits, maybe more, moving slowly, nibbling at the grass. Fab held his breath, closed his eyes and covered his ears. The echo of gunshot rippled through his body and he imagined the bullet, sharply honed in brass and steel, splitting the air on its savage journey.

* * *

When they got back to the car it was dark. His father opened the boot and slung the rabbit inside, swinging it by the ears. It smelled of musk and wild and it reminded Fab of when their old dog, Tippy, ran away and came back smelling strange, his fur wet and dark.

Fab climbed in the front beside his father, with the rifle in its warm home on the back seat, satisfied with its work. For the first time ever, his father put his arm around his shoulders and pulled him into his warmth, squeezing him just once. He smelled of pine needles and vinegar, his woollen coat hard and rough against Fab's cheek. On the way home his father didn't speak, but whistled a tune like the wind.

* * *

'Wake up!' His father shook Fab hard by the arm and he opened his eyes to the yellow light of home. 'We go in washhouse, through the back.' He thought of the washhouse with its cold, steel bench and heavy concrete trough, and he remembered the rifle, the rabbit and the blood.

Fab followed him around the narrow side of the house to the back door and, once inside, his father laid the rabbit on the bench. Its round eyes were still black and alert; it seemed almost alive but for the dark, bloody hole that punctured its chest. It was skinnier than it looked in life, still and stretched out on its side. Fab could see its bucked teeth, long and dirty. Its fur, grey and white with black flecks, looked so soft that he reached out his hand and—

'Leave it!' his father hissed, the steel in his eyes. Fab felt a sting in his belly and his face went hot. His father opened his jacket and unbuttoned a black pouch on his belt. Fab had seen the knife once before, hidden in the drawer of his father's bedside table. Its handle was as hard as stone and the blade shimmered. His father studied it, holding it up and tilting its blade to the light; then, after a deep breath in and out, he went to work.

He cut quickly and precisely, announcing each stroke, each slice of flesh, rip of skin and crunch of bone.

First we cut hees feet off
We slice hees skeen along hees belly
Loosen hees skeen from the meat
We pull hees skeen off, hees back legs first
Pull the skeen toward hees head
Like you are taking off hees jumper.

But the jumper got caught at the rabbit's head. He pulled it hard and Fab could almost feel it, like the wool his mother knitted, tight and burning on his neck and ears. He could hear tendons strain at the force centred on its spine and hear his father exhale as he sliced its head off with a flash of steel. He tossed it in the trough with the skin and fur hanging from it like a robe.

The flesh of the carcass was dark and lean: thin muscles, sinew and joints bound tight. He watched as his father sliced open its belly like an exotic fruit.

'For the dog,' he said.

He reached inside and scooped and scraped out dark organs of colours Fab had never seen. The thick velvet liver, jewels of kidney and slippery intestines slid out of the carcass and into the trough: a rich, violent stench of guts.

'We keep the liver for your mother,' he said, picking it from the pile. 'Best part, good for bolognese.'

He opened the tap, took the carcass in both hands and massaged the flesh under its flow. There was a clank of pots from the kitchen and his father's eyes smiled, the whistle of the wind returning to his lips.

* * *

The next morning, Fab rose before the light cracked over the curtains. He could still hear his father's slow, heavy snore. He felt for the plastic bag hidden under his pillow and, with it scrunched in his small fist, he lifted the blankets and stepped carefully across the floorboards to the hallway, headed for the washhouse.

Moving quietly in the quarter-light, he leaned into the trough and ran his hands down its concrete walls, feeling for the soft fur. He unravelled the bag in one hand and placed the fur inside, knotting it tightly. He found his shoes near the doorway and slipped them on. Without socks, they felt hard and unfamiliar. He moved slowly out the back door.

Outside, the air was icy and his breath steamed. He shivered as a few morning birds began a slow, throaty song. He walked down the timber ramp, then along the concrete path, past the clothesline, the plum tree, and under the arch of wet passionfruit leading to a small patch of bare earth, ready for winter planting.

He looked back to the house for any sign of movement, but its windows were still dark. Placing the bag on the ground, he knelt in the dirt and, with a trowel from the vegie patch, started to dig. The earth was soft and smelled like worms. It was easy work. Around him, the darkness was lifting and he could hear the birds shift their tone. And he could see the rabbit, dark and forlorn, with smears of blood tracing his shape against the plastic.

He put the trowel down, untied the bag and breathed in his musk. He saw his soft ears pushed into a corner, flat and low like sleep. His fur felt soft and he closed his eyes, stroking him gently with his fingertips. With both hands he lifted him out. His head hung down, eyes and mouth now closed in a dream, as he placed him lightly in the grave.

Fab sat quietly, listening to the birds and breathing the chill air, feeling the cold on his skin, and smelling the soft, wild rabbit in the moist, rich soil. Then, with his hands, he covered him in a blanket of earth.

* * *

It was a few weeks later that his father gave it to him. It was glued into the steel casing of a bullet, a coil of wire pierced through the bottom.

'It's the back one. It's special one, the left,' he said. Fab took it in his hand and felt the fur. It was stiffer than how the rabbit had felt. Prickly. 'You keep. For when you are older.'

'Look at that!' his mum said, coming in close with big eyes. 'See what your father make for you? Very lucky! You say thank you?'

Fab nodded, but all he could think of was what he buried in the yard, and that it would surely be found when his mum started digging out the potatoes.

* * *

Fab looked up to the sky, took one last drag down to the butt and stubbed the joint out on the step. He felt the rabbit's foot again.

Maybe it was lucky.

After all, his mum had never found what he'd buried – his father had decided to concrete the whole backyard early the next year. At first, he'd felt sad that the rabbit was stuck there, trapped forever under that slab. But, more than that, he felt relief that his secret was safe.

He decided that when he was feeling straight, in the morning, he'd loop another piece of wire through his key ring. Just to be safe. It might have a bit more luck left in it.

As he staggered back inside to his bedroom in the darkness, he remembered what he'd said to Lucy at the pub. He climbed into bed and the room began to gently spin.

As he lay there in the cool inky darkness, he decided that he would tell her more. About his friend. His only friend. But he would wait until they'd left town, until everything was done and they'd moved to Ballarat.

He couldn't risk things until then.

He closed his eyes and smiled – his clearest thoughts always came when he was stoned.

He knew he couldn't tell her everything, though.

There were some things that were, without doubt, better left unsaid.

Six

B en didn't come to school on the Monday.
Fab figured he was pretending to be sick. He was always sick when Burke was teaching, but it was mostly bullshit. So Fab didn't see him til Tuesday.

He ran up to him as soon as the bell went for recess, before Ben had even stood up from his desk. He poked him in the belly, a wide grin splitting his cheeks.

'What was wrong with ya?' he said.

'Nothin, had a headache.'

'Bullshit.' Fab poked him again.

'I did.'

Fab could always tell when Ben was lying – his voice would go a bit funny.

'You were just home with your horsey mag, having a good wank,' he said. 'How you gonna read it with the pages stuck together?'

Ben didn't answer, but lifted the desk lid and slid his books and pencil case inside.

'Did you get another one off him?'

'Another what?'

'One of those mags. You promised, remember?'

'Did not.' Ben stood up and headed for the door. Fab ran after him, grabbing a tennis ball from the sports kit on the way.

'Two-square?'

'Nah.'

'C'mon!'

Fab looked Ben in the eyes – they were all red and bloodshot. Maybe he really was sick after all.

'Just one game, a quick one... c'mon!'

Ben nodded. 'Okay. Just one game.'

* * *

Out on the warm, black asphalt of the schoolyard, they swatted the tennis ball gently back and forth. They always went easy for a few minutes without scoring, a warm-up before starting properly. Ben was pretty good at two-square, but Fab always felt like he had his measure.

'Burke give you a hard time about yesterday?'

Ben concentrated on the ball and didn't lift his gaze. 'Nah, not yet.'

'You got a note from ya mum?'

'Yep.'

'He's such a prick.' Fab switched and knocked the ball with his left hand. 'Do you reckon he's married or anything?'

'Who?'

'Burke.'

'Dunno.'

'Don't reckon. She'd have to be ugly.'

'I spose.'

'Kids would be ugly too. Red faces and beards, even the girls.' Fab watched Ben closely, but he didn't smile or anything. 'Well, at least it's our last year with him.'

'Yep.' Ben looped the ball into Fab's square.

'Shame it rained Saturday,' Fab said, slapping the ball back lightly with an open palm.

Ben didn't answer, but lobbed the ball back with topspin.

Fab sliced it with the back of his hand. 'That Ronnie really flipped out, didn't he?'

Ben's eyes opened wide and he swung his arm back high, whacking the ball hard down the hill, toward the oval. Fab shook his head and shot him a look – they were supposed to still be in warm-up.

Jesus, he was pissed off about something.

As he jogged after the ball, he figured maybe he should ask him what was wrong. But when he turned back, with the ball in his hand, Ben was gone.

* * *

When the bell went for lunchtime, Fab chased Ben down the main hall, past the lockers and toward the big timber doors leading out to the playground.

'Hey, what happened to you at recess?'

Ben kept walking. 'Nothin, still feel a bit sick, y'know.'

'Yeah? Well... you want half my sanga?' Fab held it out in front of him and gave it a flourish with his other hand, like they did on *Sale of the Century*. 'Salami.' He did his best Italian accent, 'Just-a-like-a-mama used to make!'

'Nah. I'm not hungry.'

'Fair enough.' Fab put the sandwich back inside its paper bag. 'Hey, I was wondering... what do you think of that Ronnie guy?'

Ben kept walking and looking straight ahead. 'He's all right.'

'Really? Ya think?'

Ben walked faster.

'Jesus Ben, will ya slow down for a sec?' Fab grabbed him by the arm, stopping him in the doorway. 'I wanna ask ya something.'

'What?'

'It's just... I've been thinking.'

'About what?'

'Well, don't you reckon it's weird about what he said?'

Ben stared past Fab, out to the oval, where some grade three girls were picking yellow flowers off the tall, green weeds.

'What was weird?' he said, his gaze still in the distance.

'Don't ya remember? In the car when we got there?'

'Nup.'

'How he knew about the Leviathan? The yabby dam?'

'Dunno.' Ben frowned and shook his head. 'Didn't really think about it.' He stared down at his feet for a second, then looked up. 'Mum told him, isn't that what he said?'

'Yeah, but did ya ask her?'

Ben shrugged. 'Nah, why would I? Who gives a shit?'

Fab had never seen Ben like this. Even that time he'd left the front gate open and Sunny ran away. He hardly ever got angry, not at anything.

'Don't you reckon he's a bit weird though? I mean...' Fab noticed Ben's eyes watering. 'Jesus Ben, what's up? Did I do something wrong or something?'

'Nuthin, just leave me alone, will ya?' Ben pushed past Fab, down the steps and ran out toward the oval.

Seven

Fab asked for permission a few days before his birthday, but his father didn't like the idea so much.

'Why you waste time with this bullshit for?' he said. 'All you need is *famiglia*. Your family, no?'

But after, when his father had gone out back, Fab's mum told him to wait. Soon, she said, his father would be going away for the weekend with Sid. She kissed him and told him to be patient. And she told him the rabbit's foot will be bringing him good luck soon and she rubbed it, then rubbed his cheeks, then kissed him again. She said it would be okay, as long as they kept it a secret.

And then Fab made her cry. But he didn't know why she got so upset. All he'd done was tell her that he loved her.

* * *

He had to wait three whole weeks before his father went away with Sid. So it was three whole weeks after his actual birthday before he could ask Ben to sleep over.

It was the first time ever, so Fab was excited. He said they'd get a video. *Die Hard*. And his mum had said that she'd make pizza.

Ben didn't look that excited though.

'I'll have to check with my mum,' he said.

The next day was a Saturday and Fab's mum told him that Ben's mum had rung and said he couldn't come, that he had chores to do or some crap. Fab's mum looked sad when she said it, but told Fab not to worry, there would be other times.

Fab thought the chores excuse was bullshit and he wondered if Ben had decided not to be his friend anymore. Maybe he just wanted to hang out at Ronnie's on weekends and look at porno mags with girls, horses and strange sex. Or maybe he just wanted to stay home and have a wank.

At first, the thought of all that made him feel a bit like he might cry. He felt sad for himself, and sad for his mum too.

But after a little while he felt angry. He was angry that Ben would choose to hang out with that weirdo instead of him.

* * *

Three weeks later, Ben had everyone's attention.

'Are you serious?' Fab said, as the boys gathered around. 'Air Max?'

'Yeah, got em yesterday. Cool, aren't they?' Ben tilted his foot to show off the air pocket near the heel.

'Yeah. Really cool.' Fab felt a wave of hot jealousy rise in him, and he wanted to stamp on Ben's feet right there. Jump on them.

'What were they,' he said, 'like, two hundred bucks?'

Johnno, being a first-class dickhead, pushed in front of Fab, knelt down and gave the air pocket a squeeze.

'Yeah, two-twenty,' Ben said.

'Jesus. You must be working hard.'

'Yeah.' He nodded. 'I spose.'

* * *

Fab waited til lunchtime to ask him. He waited til there was no one else around, when they were pissing in the urinals, just the two of them.

'How'd you pay for em?'

'What?'

Fab nodded downwards. 'The shoes, how'd you pay for em?'

Ben's face went funny, kind of tight. 'Y'know. The job.'

Fab shook his head. 'Bullshit. There's no way. That would take you like...' Fab squinted and tried to do the maths. He guessed instead. 'Ten weeks? You can't have been there that much.'

'You jealous or something?' Ben smirked and looked at Fab's shoes – Adidas Rome.

Adidas Romes had been cool in grade five. His mum had bought them without his father finding out, but said they had to last him til high school. He didn't mind that though, he knew how hard it was for her. So it hurt that Ben would make fun of them.

'Mum got these for me, Ben,' he said. 'You know that.'

Ben zipped up his trousers. 'How is she anyway?'

It was the first time Ben had asked anything about Fab's parents like that. 'Um. She's good. Why?'

'Nothin. Just asking.' He pressed the button for the flusher. 'It'd take twenty-two weeks anyway.'

'What?' The water from the flush sprayed on Fab's legs. He finished and zipped up.

'For the shoes. To pay for em. Twenty-two weeks.'

A couple of grade one kids clattered in through the doorway and Fab and Ben headed back outside.

Fab shielded his eyes as they stepped into the bright sun.

'Then how'd you pay?' he said.

'Well...' Ben stopped, looked at Fab, then let his gaze fall to the ground. 'It's kind of an advance. Ronnie reckons he'll be needing me round more often.' He paused, scraping the sole of his right shoe across the asphalt. 'Most weekends.' Ben's eyes flashed up. 'Fixing the inside of his place.'

'Most weekends?'

'Yeah.'

'Well... we won't be hanging around so much then, y'know?'

Ben brushed the dust off the sides of his shoes. 'I spose not.'

Fab felt something stir inside him, like a cold weight had been dropped in his belly. The cold moved through his body, making his limbs feel heavy and his guts sick. Time seemed to slow down and he suddenly noticed every detail – the way the sun glistened on those fancy new shoes, the smell of spilled chocolate milk going off on the asphalt, the dark emptiness in Ben's eyes – all of it burned in his mind in that brief moment.

It wasn't until years later that he would realise that the cold, twisting feeling in his guts that day was something like grief.

Eight

Ben told Fab the news at the bus stop. It was the last week of primary school and they hadn't spoken in ages. As he came close, Fab noticed how Ben had a line of dark hair above his lip. His legs looked a bit hairy too, just below the knees. On the shins, mostly.

'Hey Fab.' He had his eyes down.

'Hey.' Fab followed Ben's gaze to the ground. He stared at those shoes, still almost pristine, like he'd been extra careful not to get them dirty.

'What's that?' Ben said.

'What?'

'That.' Ben pointed at the fading yellow aura of a week-old bruise on Fab's leg. Fab thought it had completely gone.

'Fell off the fort. Last week.'

'Really? Didn't hear about that.'

'Hurt like buggery. Um, Pokey tripped me.'

'He's still givin ya trouble, or...'

'Nah. All good.'

Ben dragged a line in the dirt with his shoe. 'So, did ya hear?'

'What?'

'I'm not going to high school next year?'

'You're dropping out?'

Ben shook his head. 'Nah, I'm still goin, just not at the high school.'

'Where then?'

'Sacred Heart,' he said it so softly that Fab hardly heard.

'In Ararat?' Fab dropped his bag and crossed his arms. 'The Catholic school?'

'Yeah, Mum reckons it will be better for me.'

Better for me? *Better for me?* What the fuck did that mean?

They had always been gonna go to Stawell High together. Their plan was that Ben would let Fab copy off him so he might pass. But that plan was when they were best friends. And now everything was fucked up.

'Are you still gonna be doin stuff at Ronnie's then?' Fab said.

Ben pulled his bag tight over his shoulder and his eyes searched up the road for the bus. 'Most of it's done, he reckons.'

The bus turned the corner onto Barnes Street and began its slow, heavy grind up the hill.

'Well,' Fab said, 'maybe you'll have some more time on weekends and that.'

Ben's eyes went back to his feet and he kicked at some yellow weeds licking over the gutter from a split in the road.

'Yeah. Maybe.'

* * *

At home that night, lying in bed, Fab thought about what Ben had said. He reckoned there might be an upside. Maybe Ben might hang out a bit more from now on, especially seeing he wasn't at Ronnie's so much. And they could still be friends if they hung out on weekends. Plus, Ben could help him with some of his homework, especially if he was at a different school. No one would know if he'd copied it.

It'd be perfect.

* * *

Three days later, on the last day of school, Fab sat with some of his grade six classmates on the oval and told stories and shit, even with the girls. It felt a bit weird, but good too. Like they were older. More adult, or something.

When the bell rang for the last time, Fab went looking for Ben to see if maybe they could walk home together – he figured it would be a good time to talk about his plan. He ran around the yard, but he couldn't see him anywhere.

Then, at the front of the school, Fab spotted him. Must have left a bit early. He was already out the gate and near the bus stop with his bag. Maybe his mum was picking him up, seeing it was the last day and everything – maybe they were going to the bakery for a milkshake or something.

Fab called out, but Ben didn't hear him.

There was a beep-beep of a car horn.

Fab watched Ben jog across the nature strip as a big, shiny car swung into the kerb. But it wasn't his mum's car.

And there was still only one blue Statesman in town.

Nine

Hey, you don't look so good today. You look white, you know?' Afriki patted Fab on the shoulder. 'You sick?'

Fab was crudely attempting to dislodge a thick galvanised washer jammed in the coin slot of one of the trolleys. Sweat soaked his t-shirt.

'Self-inflicted,' he said.

Afriki slitted his eyes. 'Self in—'

'Drank too much.' The pliers slipped out of his hand. 'Fuck it!'

'Let me do this.' Afriki picked up the pliers and ushered Fab out of his way. He went to work on the washer, carefully straightening it, then giving it a sharp wiggle. He repeated the process and, within twenty seconds, he had it out.

He held the washer up to the sunlight like it was silver. 'Here. I am careful not to bend. So you still use.'

Fab took the washer and slid the pliers into his pocket. 'Beginner's luck,' he said. He turned and threw the washer across the car park, pinging it against the corrugated iron fence.

Afriki frowned. 'Why you waste? It was still good. You still can use.'

Fab shoved the trolley into the bay. 'I've got enough crap to get rid of.'

'You still have idea then, yes?'

'Selling the stuff? Yeah. The Centrelink thing was just a setback. I'll get around to it.'

'Will it take long time you think?'

'Dunno. Gotta take the pictures. Write the listings.'

Afriki slowly shook his head. 'So, maybe months then?'

Fab frowned. 'Dunno. Maybe. What's with all the questions anyway?'

'Hey, you two!' It was Dion, lighting up a smoke at the freight entrance. 'Stop yakking and do some work.'

Fab pointed at Afriki. 'He's a bad influence, boss. Won't stop talking. Always on about women.'

Afriki turned to Fab sharply. 'What you say?'

Dion put his hands on hips. 'Do something useful, will ya? Take the truck and head out to the tip. Just got a call from Cyril Magee. He's got three out there, which explains why we've been short.'

'Mystery solved then,' Fab said. 'Have you told the local rag? This is pretty big news. They'll bump their special investigation on garden-hose theft.'

Dion shook his head. 'You're so fucking funny, aren't ya, Morressi. Take Afriki with ya, so at least he knows what to do. Just in case you're not around.'

Fab raised his eyebrows. 'Am I getting promoted? You know I always wanted my picture on that board. Like a celebrity.'

Dion threw him the keys. 'Don't dick around and make sure you're back by lunchtime. I know how you like your junk.'

* * *

The tip was on the east side of town, out past Jubilee Road. That was where they built a lot of the new housing commission homes in the 1980s, little brick veneer joints mostly, each with slight variations from the one next door.

The idea was they would look like normal houses, as though no one would know the difference. To be fair, it was an improvement over the old 1960s jobs out at Stawell West, rows of identically bleak fibro boxes in shades of pastel – boiling in summer and freezing in winter.

'You like these?' Fab pointed to the houses as they passed.

Afriki nodded. 'They are nice, yes.'

'You should ask then. To get moved, I mean. The one you're in is no good.'

Afriki turned to him. 'Who I ask for this?'

Fab shrugged. 'The council maybe. I dunno. Centrelink?'

The truck shuddered loudly as it left the bitumen and hit the deep corrugations of the old track that led to the tip, effectively ending audible conversation. The road was quickly shrouded in dense, scrubby eucalypts – no one lived out this way. In a town with plenty of cheap property, land beside the tip was not the real estate of choice.

After a few kilometres, the road opened out to an expanse of cleared land. In the early eighties, the old goldmine had helped clear a few acres and dug out a landfill site. It was their way of giving some love back to the local council who had given them free rein to tunnel enormous holes beneath the town.

As a teenager, Fab would sometimes ride out there at dusk with his air rifle slung across his shoulders. The tip, at least in those days, was riddled with feral cats, some as big as a kelpie. He never managed to kill one, but he'd hit a few at least. Nowadays, you couldn't do that sort of thing – a tall cyclone fence surrounded the tip, just to make sure everyone paid the fee.

Near the entrance gate was an old shipping container that Cyril had converted into a site office. Cyril Magee was a middle-aged, grossly overweight council worker with an obsession for pornography and masturbation. The two, as he would say after a few too many at the Criterion, went 'hand in hand'.

The gate was open – they were expected. Cyril slid open the small window of his office and stuck his head out, jowly cheeks flushed with exertion.

'Cyril!' Fab called out from the truck, 'You busy in there, mate?'

Cyril pointed to the east side of the tip. 'Over there.' He slid the window shut, but Fab still heard him mutter, 'Smartarse cunt.'

Fab wound up his window, but the low, dusty stink was already inside the cabin. He laughed as he put the truck back into gear.

Afriki looked alarmed. 'Why he call you this?'

'Don't worry. He meant it with affection.'

On the east side of the tip was an assortment of car wrecks, rusted steel and general household waste. Cyril, who kept himself occupied inside his office, was less than efficient in making sure stuff got sorted.

In front of a large pile of rubbish bags were the three trolleys, waiting to be returned to their kin.

Afriki pointed at a dozen or so seagulls, circling and squawking above. 'Why are they here, so far from the sea?'

Fab shrugged. 'Dunno. Because it's such a nice spot? Or maybe they got confused by Bob's rowboat?'

'Who?'

'Never mind.'

Fab drove the truck up beside the trolleys and pulled on the handbrake, leaving the engine running. 'C'mon,' he said. 'I'll show you how to load them up.'

'Wait.' Afriki turned to him. 'I need to talk about something.'

Fab unclipped his seatbelt. 'Tell me on the way back. Much as I like it out here, I don't want you to get in trouble with Dion. You're his favourite, I reckon.'

Afriki grabbed Fab by his wrist. 'It is important.'

Fab looked at him. For the first time since he'd known him, he saw a steely seriousness in Afriki's eyes.

'Please, listen,' Afriki said.

'Okay.' He cut the engine and they sat in silence for a moment, with the low drone of blowflies as the engine cooled and ticked.

Fab was curious. Maybe Afriki had seen something? Maybe the suit had come back.

'Go on then. What is it?'

Afriki stared straight out the windscreen, watching as the seagulls circled and dived. 'I have important news.'

'Did someone come? Was someone asking about me?'

'No,' he shook his head. 'No one.'

'What then?'

He turned to Fab. 'I am leaving.'

'Leaving?' Fab frowned. 'What, the job? But you've only been doing it for—'

'No, Fab. Not just job. I leave the town. I go to Melbourne. To the Broadmeadow.'

'Broadmeadows?'

He grimaced. 'Yes, I am sorry, you say it right. The Broad-meadows.'

'But... why? Where will you stay?'

'I have job there. A cousin get for me. A factory, packing the boxes. He say it's much better money than what I get here. And not out in sun.'

Fab shook his head. 'Are you sure? I mean, Melbourne can be pretty tough you know. And Broadmeadows is a rough place.'

Afriki nodded. 'But will be good ah... the opportunity. That's what my cousin say, good opportunity. My cousin, he get me room too.'

Fab stared out to the pile of rubbish bags. Only a few of the gulls remained in the air above, circling slowly, with most having abandoned their grim quarry.

'But, this is not only thing I tell you.' Afriki put a hand on his shoulder. 'I have good news for you too, my friend.'

'What?'

Afriki was smiling, as broadly as Fab had ever seen.

'I get this job for you too.'

Ten

'W asn't expecting you this early.' Lucy was wiping down spirit bottles on the top shelf. 'You had a skinful last night.'

Fab walked to the bar. 'Paying for it. Just come in for my break. Lunch over then?'

'Yep,' she reached for a tall, dusty bottle of Galliano, unopened and seemingly untouched for decades. 'After something to eat?'

He shook his head. 'Can't stomach much today. Where's Bob?'

'Where do ya think?'

'Back playing up?'

She shrugged. 'You know the routine. Hair of the dog then?'

Fab slid onto his stool. 'Maybe just one.'

Lucy fetched a stubby from the fridge and placed it in front of him.

Fab dropped a five-dollar note on the bar. 'So,' he said, 'Afriki just gave me some news.'

'The African kid?'

'Yeah.'

Lucy crossed her arms and leaned back against the till.

'He looks like a nice boy. Always smiling. You should bring him in sometime.'

'Doesn't drink.'

'Seriously?'

'I think he's a Muslim or something. Anyway, he's got a job in Melbourne.'

She raised her eyebrows. 'Really? Good for him.'

Fab took a sip of his beer. 'Yeah, in a factory.' He put the stubby back on the bar and cleared his throat. 'He's got me a job too, if I want it.'

He paused and watched for her reaction. She flinched a little, almost imperceptibly. But he saw it.

'That right?' She tugged at the side of her apron. 'You thinking about it then?'

'Well, you know. I've got a lot on my plate and I told him that. I've gotta sell the stuff and get the house ready. Plus, I couldn't leave Mum right away. Not so suddenly. But maybe I should... you know... maybe I should think about it, at least.'

He studied her.

She nodded, her eyes thinned, but he caught something brittle in her gaze.

'You have got a fair bit on your plate,' she said. 'And you know something?'

'What?'

She glanced at his beer. 'In five years, this is the slowest I've ever seen you drink.'

The sound of heavy footsteps vibrated through the ceiling.

'Sounds like Bob's awake,' she said, looking up. 'Sure you don't want some lunch?'

Fab shook his head. 'Nah, not sure I'll finish this either.' He pushed the beer across the bar. 'Maybe I'll catch ya later on, if I'm feeling better.'

He turned for the door.

'Wait a sec,' Lucy said.

Fab looked back.

She smiled and held out the five-dollar note between her fingers. 'You didn't even drink your beer.'

'It's all right,' he said, 'you keep it.'

* * *

That afternoon, as they finished their shift, Afriki and Fab barely spoke. Fab slowly started to feel better, physically at least, as the sweat leached the previous night out of his system.

At knock off, for the first time in months, he decided he wouldn't go to the pub. He figured he needed a good night's sleep. And some time to think.

Afriki called out to him as he left the car park, 'Hey Fab. You go now?'

'Yep,' he said.

'You will think about, okay?'

'Yep, will do,' he said, without turning back.

Eleven

That night, as Fab lay in the airless heat of his room, he thought about all the junk under the house. The old timber, the ancient farm machinery, the tools and steel that had, for decades now, lain dormant. He had never really understood why his father had bought all that crap.

Maybe he had plans for something else, maybe a farm or his own business. Maybe he too had a choice, a fork in the road; maybe he had decided, without telling Fab or his mum, to start a new life somewhere without them. But he never got that chance.

As he lay there, with the sheets sticking to his skin, Fab remembered the day his father had appeared at his bedroom door.

* * *

He hadn't really seen his father, not properly, for months. They hadn't eaten a meal together since Christmas. Hadn't spoken since February.

He was supposed to be studying, but he was lying on his bed. He was thinking about Kylie Parker, who he'd pashed last week, and how cold her tongue had felt on his, like ice.

There was a knock on his door – it opened before he could answer.

His father stood there, silent in the doorway, deep breaths in and out.

He had once been a giant, broad and tall for his generation, densely muscular. Big, strong hands and long, sinewy arms – a powerful neck and jutting Roman jaw. He'd exuded a primal strength, as though he'd not sprung from humankind, but something supernatural, almost unholy – something not of this earth.

And he'd moved and acted like a man who knew, always, that his prowess exceeded all others.

But he had changed.

In the doorway he stood, wearing loose, black woollen pants, a thick brown belt and white shirt, unbuttoned to his chest. His skin had a greyish hue, but shone strangely in Fab's room, like a flame still burned deep within him, glowing through a fog.

None of his clothes seemed to fit, they looked like hand-me-downs – all wrong, oversized. Where once his shoulders were round and rippling, angled bones now poked through cotton. Where once his legs had been like stone pillars, the wool hung drab and loose to his battered boots. Where once his face was wide, proud and bright, his skin sat thin and sallow against his cheekbones.

All his sinew and strength had been eaten away. It seemed, in the end, only the skeleton would triumph, rising up like an ancient shipwreck, a relic – the final remnant of a deep and unknowable ocean.

His father stood in the doorway, breathing roughly.

'Your mother tell you?' he said, his eyes fierce and shining darkly.

Fab shook his head.

'I am dying, Fabri. A few weeks.'

Fab nodded.

'You understand?'

Fab looked at him.

And said nothing.

His father stayed for a moment longer, silent but for the quiet whistle of his breath, with an eternity stretching out between them.

Then he turned and closed the door gently behind him.

* * *

The day after the funeral, Fab went out into the Black Ranges with his father's rifle, the Beretta, slung over his shoulder. He sat in a field of yellow grass at the foot of the tallest hill and laid it down by his side. He unbuttoned the case, slowly, and lifted it from its soft, warm home. It looked different in the light. The maple seemed a brighter yellow and the steel of the barrel held the lustre of deep, polished ebony.

He leaned back into the grass, felt the sun on his skin, and breathed in deeply. He closed his eyes and remembered. The smell of earth, pine needles and vinegar.

As the sun slowly sank behind the ranges, a chill came to the air and he knew he didn't have much time. He put the rifle carefully back inside its soft leather case, buttoned it, and marched quickly up the hill. He had a rough idea where it was, a hundred metres or so up, but he wasn't sure he'd be able to find it.

It was almost dark and Fab thought he must have misjudged the distance, or maybe it had been filled in. But then, just as he was about to give up, he found the spot, just off the track in a small clearing shrouded by thick shrubs. On an old gum tree, someone had nailed a sheet of rusted iron, with 'DANGER' daubed in dark red paint.

'The deepest mineshaft in Victoria,' his father would say, with pride in his eyes. When they went hunting he would warn Fab to be careful, to make sure he didn't fall in. And Fab imagined that it must have gone almost to the centre of the earth.

Fab walked to the edge of that deep black hole and felt the cool, damp air on his skin. He wondered how far it went down... twenty, maybe thirty metres? Deep enough.

He breathed in the air, lifted the rifle up over the shaft and, with his eyes closed, he let it fall from his hands. It clanked once, then again a second later, but he never heard it land.

Then, with his eyes still closed, he reached into his pocket for the rabbit's foot and gripped it tightly in his hand, pushing it deeper, safer, inside his coat.

* * *

And now, eleven years later, as he lay in his bed waiting for sleep, he thought about all that junk his father had left behind. How it lay there under the house, the remnants of the past they had all shared. How he planned to sell it, to turn a profit, to make some good out of the ruins.

And it occurred to him, in those flickering seconds before sleep, in a moment of terrible clarity he would never fully recall, that all that junk was the embodiment of his past.

Bent, broken, rusted, and mostly worthless.

Twelve

He knew the pub wouldn't be open yet. And he knew there was a definite risk of running into Bob. But soon enough, as far as he could tell, none of that would matter.

He waited under a tree in the rear car park. Bob had planted a whole lot of trees out there when he first bought the place, but only a few had survived. He'd even put a few tables and chairs out for a beer garden, but never got the liquor permit for it.

It was Wednesday. And Fab knew that on Wednesday, Lucy got the beer delivery from Melbourne. He knew Lucy got it because the supermarket got it right after and the truck driver, Mick, a heavily tattooed Pentridge graduate, would tell Fab all the imaginative ways he would like to fuck her.

Eventually, at around ten-thirty, the truck rounded the corner. It honked its air horn on the way in and, after just a few moments, Lucy emerged through the back door. She didn't see Fab as he waited in the shade.

He watched her make small talk with Mick, flashing a bright and easy grin. She then unlocked the cellar door while Mick knelt down, apparently checking his tyre pressure, but instead looking up her skirt.

Mick then unloaded the barrels through the door. Fab

watched as each of them fell on an old car tyre, then bounced and clunked noisily within. Lucy once told Fab that when she first started, Bob used to wait down there, rolling and stacking the barrels neatly into place. But from the day they got married, even that job was left to her.

When Mick was done, he fetched the delivery book from the front seat of his truck. Lucy signed, smiled, and handed it back. Mick lingered for a moment, hands on hips. Fab couldn't hear what was being said, but Lucy wasn't smiling anymore. Mick reached out for her hand, but she pulled away.

After what seemed like forever, Mick slowly got back in his truck and started it up. And Fab made his move.

'Lucy!' he called out from under the tree, but she didn't hear him above the rumble of the engine. She headed for the door.

'Lucy!' he yelled out this time. She turned and looked at the truck, frowning. Then Fab stepped out from the shade.

'Fab?' She shook her head and squinted into the light. 'Why are you hiding over there?'

He walked to her.

'Making sure you don't get abducted by Mr Milat.'

She rolled her eyes. 'You won't believe what he said.'

'Don't wanna know.'

Lucy looked him up and down. 'Well now! Don't you look smart? Don't think I've ever seen you in a shirt.'

He shrugged. 'Gotta make an effort sometimes.'

'Like a magpie in spring! How come you're not at work?'

His heart pounded. He suddenly had the vague, uneasy feeling of being slightly outside himself, of looking on.

'Well, that's kinda why I'm here,' he said.

'What do you mean?'

'I ah... I'm about to quit.'

Lucy crossed her arms. 'You serious? But you've never even missed a day in—'

'Years, I know. But I... I've been thinking about things.' He swallowed drily. 'And I... I think I'm gonna take the job.'

'In Melbourne?'

'Yeah. The factory. Afriki.'

Her mouth fell open just a little. 'But, I thought you said...'

'I know. But I... I thought about things and I realised I need to bite the bullet, you know? I can't just keep waiting for things to happen.'

'But what about your plan?' She frowned. 'All that stuff?'

He shrugged. 'I'll just sell the place. Lock, stock and barrel. Whoever buys it can deal with it. Take it to the tip if they want.'

'Your mum?'

'I'll get her a little unit in town, closer to everything. She'd be happier, I reckon.'

Lucy shook her head. 'I... I just didn't think that you'd ever...'

'There's one other thing though...'

He looked down at the gravel, dragging a line in the dirt with his shoe. He could hear, off in the distance, the hiss of brakes as Mick's truck pulled up at the supermarket.

'I um...' He sucked a deep breath in and out. 'Um...'

'What?'

He bit his lip. 'I... I wondered if... if ah... if maybe you might want to come...' He looked her in the eyes. 'Maybe... um... come with me.'

Fab knew that he'd said it. There was no one else who could have. But the voice sounded alien to his ears, distant. And the words hung dangerously in the air.

She didn't blink for a long time. She stared at him, her mouth opening and closing, but with no sound.

Eventually, she spoke.

'Fab... I... I can't just go. I mean. It's not that easy.'

'But you... you always planned to go to Melbourne, remember?'

'I know... but...'

He scraped another line in the gravel with his shoe. 'You don't need to decide right now, but...'

'I just...'

'I know the factory job might not be the greatest. But it's just a start, you know? No more working like a slave for Bob. No more of the dickheads in this town. Just me and you.'

She shook her head. 'I just can't. I mean... Bob's not perfect, but...'

'It won't be easy at the beginning I know, but—'

Her voice cracked. 'It's not so simple.' Two tears rolled violently down her cheeks.

Fab took hold of her hand. 'You don't need to decide now. Just think about it.'

'I don't think I'll change my mind, Fab. It's just—'

'Sleep on it.'

She took a deep breath in and out. She looked him in the eyes, then glanced back at the pub. She leaned in and kissed him quickly on the lips.

'I better head back in.'

He held fast to her hand. 'Promise me you'll think about it.'

She tried to pull away. 'I'm sorry, Fab.'

'Please. Promise.'

She let out a deep sigh. 'Okay. I promise.'

He let her go.

He stayed there and watched her walk quickly across the car park. She didn't turn back. He closed his eyes for a moment. He just needed to shut out that bright, harsh sun. He needed some kind of relief.

But he couldn't, as much as he tried, close out the sound of the door slamming shut.

Thirteen

A friki stared at Fab like a long-lost brother.
'Dion tell me you are sick.' He shoved a trolley into the bay and looked Fab up and down. 'But I never see you so... dressed like a... like a gentleman!'

Fab leaned over the trolley bay. 'It's an important day.'

Afriki looked toward the supermarket, then back to Fab. 'If Dion see you here... he is very angry you didn't come to work.'

Fab shrugged. 'He better get used to it.'

'What do you mean?'

He smiled. 'What do you think I mean?'

Afriki's eyes widened. 'You mean... you will come?'

'Just need to sort a couple of things. But I can tell you now,' he shook his head, 'I definitely won't be doing this shit anymore.'

Afriki rushed to him and shook his hand. 'You make right decision, my friend. The right decision!'

'Hey Morressi!' Dion strode across the car park. 'I thought you were sick?'

'I recovered.'

'You came to work, or just to distract my star employee?'

'Neither. I'm calling it quits.'

'What? For good?'

'Yep.'

'Is that right?' Dion crossed his arms. 'What's brought this on?'

Fab shrugged. 'You think this is tough to leave?'

'You been here a while though, Fab. How long you reckon?'

'You would know.'

'Well, it will break my heart to see you go. But I can easy get another darkie in to replace ya.'

'You're all class.'

Dion lit a smoke and nodded toward the Criterion over the road. 'Hasn't got anything to do with that little slut, has it?'

Fab darkened. 'Watch your mouth.'

'Mate, you never learn, do ya? Still thinking with your dick.' He grinned. 'C'mon Afriki, back to it, mate.'

Afriki whispered, 'I call my cousin tonight. I tell him we both come. I tell Dion tomorrow and we talk then, yes? We have much to plan.'

'Afriki!' Dion yelled.

Fab smiled. 'Sounds good.'

* * *

As Fab headed back out into the street, he glanced over to the Criterion, which still hadn't opened. Even though things hadn't gone exactly to plan, he hoped Lucy would come around. Like him, she just needed some time to think. It wasn't something you could decide on the spot. At least she knew now that he was serious, that it wasn't just some pipe dream.

For the first time he could remember, he felt like he was taking charge of things. He was making decisions. It felt good.

As he walked down the street, he heard the low, throaty rumble of a V8 starting up – he'd recognise that sound anywhere, the rough, lusty gurgle of a big, thirsty engine. He turned back, but couldn't see anything – not in the car park, or on the street. So he kept walking, turned the corner, and headed up Barnes Street toward home.

Then, up ahead, near the cemetery, a dark blue Commodore entered the roundabout and turned right, toward him. It wasn't a car he'd seen in town before, but he figured it must be the V8 he'd just heard.

As it approached, it slowed right down, like it was about to stop beside him, before speeding up again. He tried to see who was driving, but its windows were darkly tinted.

And he wondered, for a brief moment, if maybe WorkCover were still on his tail.

And he smiled as he realised something – he just didn't care about that anymore.

Fourteen

Whack! Whack! Whack!

Fab woke and felt the hot burn of bile rising in his throat. What was that noise? He propped himself up on his elbows and tried to open his eyes. Bright sun. Too much for a first attempt. He lay back down, closed his eyes and waited for the powerful tide of nausea to recede.

Whack! Whack! Whack!

There it was again.

'Muuum!' he called out.

No answer.

He reached blindly for his phone and flicked it open. 10.46 am. Shit. Already late for work and... then, he remembered.

Whack! Whack! Whack!

The door.

'Coming!' His mouth was dry. He swallowed with a dull click.

He sat up on the edge of the bed, naked – the room surged and rolled and he had to steady himself on the mattress. He picked up a glass of water from the floor and swallowed it in one gulp. Little improvement.

He'd planned just a few quiet ones at home. To celebrate. He couldn't go to the Criterion – he needed to give Lucy some space – even though every part of his entire being wanted to see her, to be near her, to convince her.

But it was like magic – the more he drank, the less he felt that urge. So a few quiet ones became a few more and—

Whack! Whack! Whack!

'Yeah, I said I'm coming!'

His voice sounded deep. In spite of how shit he felt, he kind of liked it. He remembered that after he finished his beers he had a joint as well, a biggie. It seemed like a good idea at the time. He remembered having a dream about primary school, being out on the hot asphalt, and the taste of sour milk.

Whack! Whack! Whack!

'Just hold on, will ya?'

As he pulled on his jeans, he wondered who it could be. Then he remembered. Afriki. He said they needed to talk, plan things out. But Fab was in no fit state for that conversation – Afriki would have to come back later. Maybe tomorrow.

He found a white singlet on the floor and sniffed it. Maybe on its third day, which was still fine.

He stood up. A little too quickly. The room heaved left and right, his head throbbed and he sat back down on the bed, the saliva thick in his mouth.

Then it came back to him.

Out in the car park. His hand on hers. He made her promise.

He stood up, swallowed down the saliva and raced toward the front door, bouncing off each side of the hallway wall as he went.

He opened the door and squinted, his hand shielding the morning sun. His eyes slowly adjusted.

It wasn't what he had hoped for.

Behind the flyscreen, standing on the steps, was a man in a dark suit.

Fab pushed the flyscreen open.

'Good morning,' the man said.

'Morning.'

'Fabrizio Morressi?'

The man spoke carefully, even pronouncing his surname just right. Morr-*essi*, not Morrissey. No one around town ever got that right.

Fab sighed. 'Look, I know what this is about. I don't care about the WorkCover. Cut me off if you want.'

The man frowned. 'I don't know anything about that, Mr Morressi.'

'Look, I'm pretty busy right now, so—'

'I'm Detective Senior Constable Mackie.'

Fab shook his head. 'What's this all about?'

'Mr Morressi, we think you might be able to help us with something. Something we found in the river.'

Part Three

Part Three

One

This is a recording of an interview between myself, Detective Senior Constable Vincent Mackie, and Mr Fabrizio Morressi, conducted at the Stawell Police Station on Tuesday the thirteenth of May, 2006. Additional persons present are corroborator, Detective Sergeant David Mullins.

VM: Mr Morressi, do you agree that the time is now 11.35 am?

FM: Yes.

VM: Can you state your full name and address please?

FM: Fabrizio Morressi. Eight McLaughlin Street, Stawell West.

VM: Now I must inform you that you are not obliged to say or do anything, but anything you say or do may be given in evidence. Do you understand that?

FM: Yes.

VM: I must also inform you of the following rights. You may communicate with or attempt to communicate with a friend or a relative to inform that person of your whereabouts. You may communicate with or attempt to communicate with a legal practitioner. Do you wish to exercise any of these rights before we proceed?

FM: Ah... no.

VM: What is your age and date of birth?

FM: Twenty-eight years old. Thirteenth of June, 1977.

VM: Are you an Australian citizen?

FM: Yes.

VM: Are you an Aboriginal or Torres Strait Islander?

FM: No.

VM: Mr Morressi, do you know of a Mr Ronald Bellamy, formerly of Navarre Road in Stawell?

FM: Yes, I um... knew of him.

VM: How well did you know Mr Bellamy?

FM: Not very well.

VM: How did you know him then?

FM: He lived a few doors up from a friend. Years ago though. When I was a kid.

VM: Who was that friend?

FM: Ben.

VM: Ben? What was his surname?

FM: Carver. Ben Carver.

VM: Was that at... 159 Patrick Street?

FM: Ben or Bellamy?

VM: Um, Bellamy.

FM: 159... could be, yeah. Never paid attention to numbers.

VM: Do you know who lived there before?

FM: At Bellamy's?

VM: Yes.

FM: Um, I think it was the Wolfes. Daisy, Joe and their parents. Daisy's dead though, she—

VM: Yes, we know about Daisy. Did you know Percy Wolfe? Her father?

FM: Not really. I mean, I knew who he was. But I didn't know him, if you know what I mean.

VM: Okay. And so the Wolfes moved out?

FM: Yes.

VM: And Mr Bellamy moved in.

FM: That's usually how it goes.

VM: But Percy Wolfe continued to own the property, didn't he?

FM: I wouldn't know.

VM: Well, I can tell you that he did. And that he rented it to Mr Bellamy.

FM: Okay. But so what?

VM: Did you have much contact with Mr Bellamy while he lived there?

FM: Not really. Ben probably had more to do with him.

VM: Mr Carver?

FM: Yep. Ben.

VM: And is Mr Carver still living in town?

FM: No.

VM: Do you know where he is nowadays?

FM: No. I mean, it's been a long time, you know. Haven't seen him since we were kids.

VM: And when was the last time you saw him?

FM: Ben?

VM: Yes.

FM: Exactly?

VM: If you can remember, yes.

FM: Jeez, not for years. You're testing my memory. Not since primary school, I reckon. He kinda disappeared, you know?

VM: Disappeared?

FM: I ah... yeah. I mean, I just never saw him again.

VM: You didn't see him after primary school?

FM: He was gonna go to high school in Ararat, last I heard.

VM: So the last time you saw him was?

FM: Last day of primary school, I reckon. For certain, now I think about it.

VM: Never saw him again after that?

FM: Didn't I just say that? Listen, can I get a glass of water or something?

VM: Ah yeah, sure. Dave – can you...? Yeah, maybe a jug. Interview suspended at 11.43 am.'

Two

Fab put on his favourite jacket. It was the first thing he bought with his pay that year – the last year of high school.

It was a brown corduroy bomber with woollen lining. In it, he was invincible.

The job at the supermarket was tough, but it gave him an advantage over the smarter and better-looking boys at school – it gave him money. He could buy clothes, a shit-box '77 Chrysler Sigma, booze, smokes and dope.

'Where are you going tonight?' his mum called out. The TV was loud. He heard the gong of 'Red Faces'. Her favourite.

He adjusted the collar in the bathroom mirror. Up or down? Down. Up looked a bit try-hard.

'I told ya. Brad Perry's.'

'Who?'

'Brad Perry!'

'Where?'

'At his farm.'

Silence, as there always was before the next question.

'Will there be drinking?'

'Dunno, Mum. Maybe.' Fab opened the medicine cabinet and grabbed his stash, hidden in a roll of old footy strapping tape.

'You eat? There's bolognese on the stove.'

'Later.'

'Whose party is it again?'

'I told ya, Brad Perry's.'

It was the last week of high school and Fab wasn't planning on coming home that night.

Brad Perry's parties were the stuff of legend. He was a thirty-year-old guy with a panel van, ponytail and an obsession with high-school girls. Basically, he was a dick. But he threw great parties – bands, DJs, lighting – the works. At last year's party, he'd even got strippers down from Ballarat. This year, who knew?

Another clang of the 'Red Faces' gong.

He carefully moulded his hair with gel, gently lifting the fringe into a small wave, before checking both sides with the hand mirror. He wanted it perfect tonight. Holly would be there.

Holly Kilpatrick was from Ararat. She had blonde hair down to her arse, a wide brown face and full lips. Her tits weren't that big, but they were hard, almost muscular, and when Fab had licked at her nipples she'd squealed. And anyone from out of town, even just Ararat, seemed kind of exotic.

'Be careful,' his mum said, without shifting her gaze from the telly.

'Don't worry. I won't be late.'

* * *

The party was on a bush block about five kilometres out of town. At the edge of the block was dense, dark scrub where people would go to piss or fuck, but the ground there was uneven and got trickier as the night went on.

That was where Fab hid his booze, in a cooler bag under a white gum tree; he knew he'd remember that, even when he was bent.

'Fuck mate, watch where you're goin!'

He careened into a group of metal-heads. It was just after one o'clock. The party was really kicking off.

'My fault!' He held his hands up. 'Sorry dudes!'

He stumbled away, checked his jeans for the dope and felt the foil crinkle in his fingers. One more drink, then he'd light up. It always made things a bit easier.

He strode through the long grass, reached into his pocket and pulled out his smokes. Benson and Hedges. In year eleven, he'd given up the Peter Jacksons. These ones seemed classier, with the gold packet, but not as poncy as Dunhills. He searched his pocket for a lighter, but instead his fingers found the tattered rabbit's foot, chained to his key ring.

There was a cheer as the opening riff from 'Smells Like Teen Spirit' rippled through the chill night air. He found the cooler bag behind the tall white tree where he'd left it. Two cans left. He couldn't think how many he'd had. Seven? Jesus. Couldn't have. Maybe someone nicked some. He decided to drink one and put the other in his coat pocket for safekeeping.

'Hey Fab!' Someone lurched at him through the gloom. 'Got a light?'

It was Dion Shea. He was zipping up his jeans after taking a piss. Dion worked at the supermarket too, but he was in the deli, which was a bit more senior. He was a dick, but Fab put up with him, mostly because he would 'accidentally' cut extra slices of ham for Fab to make his lunch.

'Nah, lookin for one too.' Fab scanned the crowd for the telltale red embers. There was a group of older guys smoking near the DJ booth, but they'd tell him to get fucked for sure. The natural order of things.

'Over there,' Dion said, pointing to a lone figure near the farm gate, where a flicker of light flashed and vanished.

They walked toward it, swaying into each other on the way. Fab didn't like the idea of Dion hanging around; he was baggage, sleazy, and girls generally hated him. He'd ditch him as soon as he could.

'Gonna pull tonight, Fab?'

'Dunno, might head home soon if—'

'If what?' Dion laughed. 'If Kilpatrick doesn't show up? Jesus, you're fuckin hopeless.'

He glared. 'Is that right?'

Dion poked him in the ribs. 'Stop thinking with your dick. It's just a root, remember? All pretty much the same.'

'Like you'd know.'

'She's got a boyfriend too, lover-boy!'

He knew she had a boyfriend – 'Chinga' Moloney. His real name was Louis, but they called him Chinga because he had eyes like a Chinaman. Fab heard he had been locked up at Turana for bashing his woodwork teacher. He also heard he was kind of like a pit-bull, but more violent.

'Hey mate, can we get a light?'

Dion announced their approach to the smoker, who was leaning back against the gate. A taxi pulled in the driveway and its headlights shone from behind, making him look like something from the *X-Files*. He was tall, muscular, but there was something stiff about the way he stood. It put Fab on edge. He squinted and shielded his eyes from the headlights. The smoker reached into his pocket, pulled out a book of matches and threw them to Dion.

'Is that you, Fab?' the smoker said. Fab couldn't place the voice.

'Maybe.'

He tried to make out the face in the gloom. He clenched his fist. If it was Chinga, best to get one good punch in, then run. It was important to know your limitations.

Dion passed the matches to Fab. Behind the gate, the taxi reversed back down the driveway, its lights drawing into the night.

Fab lit up and kept his eyes on the smoker.

'Don't you recognise me?' he said, crunching a cigarette under his foot. The lights from the party flashed red and green, then broke into a bright blue strobe as a heavy bassline kicked in. It shone in flickering bands across the smoker – first his legs, then his torso, and finally his face.

As Fab inhaled the smoke deeply into his lungs, he looked into those dark eyes and a smile turned the corners of his mouth.

A soothing warmth, a feeling he hadn't known in so long, flooded through him; it was heavy and it was deep and it was something like home.

Three

After the second joint, Fab felt it coming. He ran to the side of the road with the whole world rolling like the ocean and his mouth full of spew.

He heaved the contents of his belly – bourbon and cola – and felt only slightly better.

Ben laughed. 'Jesus, how much did you drink?'

Fab spat and wiped his mouth with his sleeve. 'Not that much.' He shivered as the wind sliced through his clothes. He longed for bed. The party had ended after the police rocked up and shut down the music. No strippers. No Holly Kilpatrick.

He staggered to the middle of the road.

'How long you reckon it's gonna take us?' Ben said.

'Dunno. Twenty minutes maybe?' Fab angled his watch to the moonlight. 'Three-thirty now, so I reckon we'll be back in town by four at the latest.'

The road twisted through the Black Ranges – no one used it anymore, except farmers. It was broken and cracked, with potholes that would never be filled, especially since the bypass was built.

The half-moon shone just enough light to reveal their path, winding through a dense forest of ironbark. It suddenly felt like a long way back to town. Fab knew the way by daylight, he'd been up here yabbying more times than he could remember, but at night everything looked different.

'Maybe someone will give us a lift?' he said.

'Everyone was drinking.' Ben shook his head. 'I wouldn't get in.'

Fab pulled his jacket collar up against the wind. 'Yeah, good call.' If anyone offered a lift, he'd have said yes in a heartbeat. 'How'd you go with year twelve anyway?'

'Okay, I think.' Ben shrugged. 'Not many of us left in the end.' He pulled up the hood of his coat.

'What d'ya mean?'

'Half the girls got knocked up. The boys dropped out to work on farms, or go on the dole.'

Fab wondered if he'd have been better to drop out himself. Year twelve felt like a waste of time. Could have got some extra shifts at the supermarket. If he played his cards right, Dion reckoned he might be able to get him a spot in the deli.

'So you goin to uni then?' Fab said.

'Gonna try, yeah. What about you?'

Fab shot him a look.

Ben laughed. 'Fair enough.' He pointed up the road. 'Hey, look where we are.'

Fab could see what Ben was pointing at. Twenty metres or so up ahead the moonlight shone on water, as flat and still as glass.

The old Leviathan dam.

'Shit,' Fab said. 'Haven't been here in years.'

The Leviathan was on the edge of the ironbark forest and was shielded from the north, but a cold southerly blew in like ice. The wind gusted and Fab pulled his jacket in tighter. 'They reckon it's polluted as fuck now,' he said, 'from the mine. Remember how we used to come yabbying here?'

'Course I do. I always did better though. You and your dog food...'

Fab laughed. 'It was a good system! That used to be so much fun though. We had good times, didn't we?'

'Was great.'

'I miss that sometimes.'

They stood in silence for a moment and Fab suddenly wished he hadn't said it, even though it was true. Then Ben spoke, slowly and carefully, like he'd been thinking about it for a while.

'I heard about your dad.'

The wind whistled through the trees and the thick branches moaned in the darkness. Fab swallowed and his throat clicked drily. He reached for the last of the dope in his pocket.

'It was for the best.'

He pushed his hand deeper and felt for the rabbit's foot, bony and dry against his fingertips.

'Must have been tough,' Ben said.

Fab let out a deep breath. 'He was pretty brutal.' He looked at Ben, his eyes sparkling in the moonlight. 'You remember, don't ya?'

Ben nodded.

'I um... I'll never forget what you did for me back then.'

'What do ya mean?'

The wind whistled once more through the trees.

Fab shrugged. 'By being normal about everything. Being my friend and that.'

'Forget it. How's your mum going?'

Fab felt his chest go tight. An old, strong current had begun to flow again inside him, pulling him deep. He couldn't keep talking about that stuff. Not his mum and dad. Not now.

'She's good. But that's enough heart-to-heart.' He held up the foil – it glistened in the blue-grey light of the moon. 'What do ya reckon?'

'Another one? I dunno Fab, I—'

'C'mon, for old time's sake. Might warm us up.' Fab moved up close and slung an arm around Ben, squeezing him tight. 'I don't see you that often y'know, and if you're going to uni next year to become a big-shot...'

Ben smiled, easily wrestling loose from Fab's grip. 'Yeah, all right then. Just for old time's sake.'

* * *

Fab sat on the ground at the bottom of a gatepost, with his body shielding the dope from the wind. Ben climbed the old steel gate and perched on top, his legs dangling and his thick, woollen duffle coat wrapped around him like a blanket.

Fab rolled the joint carefully. He was happy with his efforts – nice and tight, but loose enough to let the air through; he was definitely getting better at it. He lit up, took a hard drag, and passed it to Ben.

'Nah, have a couple more. I'm pretty ripped already.' Ben swung his legs from side to side, clapping his boots together.

Fab stood up, leaned against the gate and looked out over the water. He took another drag and blew out a thick plume of blue smoke that whipped back into his face, stinging his eyes.

'Hey, I just thought of something. Remember that girl, Daisy? The clothesline and all that?'

Ben stopped swinging his legs and didn't say anything for a second. 'Yeah.'

'Remember how we wondered why she did it?'

'Yeah.'

'Dion Shea reckons he knows.'

Ben pushed his hands into his pockets. 'That right?'

'Apparently her dad was porking her. Can you believe it?'

Ben hopped down from the gate. 'Dion Shea is full of shit.'

Fab shrugged. 'He said a friend of the family told him. Parents are split up now.' He took a long drag. 'Fuck, this is strong. Must be the stuff from up north.' He watched Ben kicking at the dirt. 'Hey, remember that guy up the road from your joint?'

'Who?'

'That guy with the car. What's his name? Ronnie.'

Ben stopped and turned around. Fab sucked in the last of the dope in a bright flare.

'He was weird, wasn't he?'

Ben stared at him for a moment, then walked a few steps back up toward the road, the gravel crunching as he went.

'We'd better keep moving,' he said, 'otherwise we'll never get back.'

'Hold on a sec,' Fab followed him up the driveway.

Ben kept walking toward the road. 'C'mon, let's get going,' he said. 'It's cold.'

'Hang on a minute.' Fab flicked the butt into the bushes. 'Remember when he took us yabbying? How he knew about this place?'

Ben stopped walking, like he was about to turn around, but then kept going. Faster.

'Ben,' Fab ran up and grabbed him by the arm. 'Will ya stop?'

Ben turned back, his face hard and twisted, and swung his elbow deep into Fab's chest.

Fab dropped to his knees, with spit dripping from his lips. '*Fuck!*' He hunched over, braced his ribs and gasped for air.

He looked up the road and watched as Ben disappeared into the darkness.

Four

Interview resumed at 11.55 am. Present are Mr Fabrizio Morressi, Detective Sergeant David Mullins and myself, Detective Senior Constable Vincent Mackie. Okay, so I'd like to ask a few more questions about Mr Bellamy.

FM: Righto.

VM: Did he ever come to your house?

FM: No.

VM: Did you ever go there?

FM: ...

VM: For the benefit of the recording, Mr Morressi?

FM: Sorry, no. I never went to Bellamy's.

VM: What about your friend, Ben Carver. Did he ever go there?

FM: He did a few chores and stuff like that, from memory. Mowing the lawn and that kind of shit. Then he might have moved, I think.

VM: Bellamy?

FM: Yeah.

VM: Was that to... Navarre Road?

FM: No idea.

VM: Did you know where he worked?

FM: Why would I?

VM: Maybe just answer the question.

FM: He might have worked at the mine. Can't be sure though – a lot of people worked at the mine. People passing through.

VM: And Mr Bellamy was from out of town, wasn't he?

FM: Don't know. Like I said, Ben knew him better than me.

VM: Did you know where he was from?

FM: I don't know. Melbourne maybe? Look... I'm not sure why you're asking me about this, I—

VM: We just need some information. To help us clarify a few things.

FM: Yeah, but I'm not sure what any of this has got to do with me.

VM: We'll come to that.

FM: Is it gonna take much longer? I'm expecting someone at home and I—

VM: Just concentrate on the questions. Did you know he was from interstate?

FM: Who?

VM: Mr Bellamy.

FM: No, I told ya I didn't know.

VM: Did Mr Carver know?

FM: How should I know?

VM: Well, I can inform you that he came from interstate. He was from South Australia. And before that, Queensland. And before that, New South Wales.

FM: So?

VM: He was also known by a different name. Mr Frank Steers. Did you know he'd been to jail in the past, Mr Morressi?

FM: No, look I told you I hardly knew him. I was just a kid, you know?

VM: Well, he had been in jail a number of times. Mostly for sex offences against children. He is also a person of interest in a number of disappearances.

FM: Well... there's a lot of weirdos around, isn't there?

VM: Did you know that Mr Bellamy and Mr Wolfe knew each other?

FM: Well, you said he rented off him so...

VM: That's not what I meant. Did you know they had been friends for many years? That they had worked together?

FM: No.

VM: Did you know they had lived together, interstate?

FM: ...

VM: Mr Morressi?

FM: No.

VM: No what?

FM: No... I didn't know they... that they lived together.

VM: Mr Morressi, this may be difficult for you to answer, but did Mr Bellamy or Mr Wolfe ever have any inappropriate contact...

FM: Inappropriate contact?

VM: With you. Anything ah... sexual.

FM: No. Absolutely... no. Definitely not.

VM: Nothing sexual at all? No touching? Anything like that?

FM: No. No way.

VM: And what about your friend. Mr Carver?

FM: ...

VM: Mr Morressi, what about Ben Carver? Your friend?

FM: I um... I don't think so. Not that he said. I mean, I wouldn't really know, would I?

VM: Well, was Ben at his house very often?

FM: Just for the jobs. The mowing and that, like I said.

VM: How often was that?

FM: Dunno. Once a month maybe?

VM: And did Mr Bellamy ever take Mr Carver anywhere else?

FM: I... don't know. Maybe. Maybe just once. Once that I remember.

VM: And what happened that time, Mr Morressi?

FM: I don't really know. I mean... we'd been yabbying. All three of us.

VM: Bellamy too?

FM: Yeah, he took me and Ben to his block out at Glenorchy.

VM: And then?

FM: I got dropped home. VM: And what about Ben?

FM: He went with Bellamy. He was supposed to take him home, but...

VM: He didn't take him home?

FM: I'm not... I don't think so, no.

VM: Do you know what happened when he went with Bellamy?

FM: Not at the time I didn't... I mean, not exactly. He said he was going to drop him home, but I didn't know so I...

VM: You say "not at the time".

FM: Yeah.

VM: What did you find out later, Mr Morressi?'

Five

Ronnie said the shack was his secret. He said it wasn't on a farm or anything and the trees surrounded it completely, so you wouldn't even know it was there. He said it wasn't too far, so it wasn't gonna take long. He just needed to get his tools.

Once they got out of town, Ronnie turned off the highway and they were on a dirt road for a long time. As they went further into the Black Ranges, the trees got thicker and closer as the road narrowed. Ben had never been there before, but he knew Fab went there with his dad sometimes.

It wasn't til they were a long way out that Ronnie spoke. 'So how'd you like that magazine I gave ya?'

Ben felt the blood rush to his face. 'It's all right.' He crossed his arms. 'Good, I mean.'

'Yeah?' Ronnie had a big grin. 'What bits did you like?'

Ben wasn't sure what to say and he tried not to think about the weird picture.

'The girls, I spose.'

'You spose?' Ronnie laughed. 'What did you like about them?'

'I dunno.' Ben's heart pounded. 'Their boobs and that.'

'Yeah, some good tits all right.' Ronnie got his smokes out from the console. 'Did ya like what was being done to them?'

Ben thought about the red faces, the sweat, the big veiny dicks and how the girls looked in pain.

'Yeah,' he said.

Ronnie lit a smoke and powered down the window, the cool air rushed inside and was a relief on his skin. Ronnie took a long drag and blew the smoke out sideways.

'Would you like to do that to them?' he said.

Ben looked at the glove box, with its round steel lock and its leather trim. He wondered what was inside it and what sort of key opened it and he wished like anything that Ronnie would stop talking.

'I spose.'

'How's it make you feel when you think about it?' Ronnie spoke more softly, and Ben could hardly hear him above the wind rushing in.

'I dunno.' He fumbled at the buckle of his seatbelt, looking at the shiny chrome, rubbing his fingers against it. 'I like it, I spose.'

Ronnie got a big smile on his face again. 'Fair enough. Well, I might have some more mags for you up at the shack. What d'ya reckon?'

Ben didn't really want any more of them. He was worried enough that his mum might find the one he had. But he'd be happy if he could get just one more, just one more for Fab.

'Yeah, maybe.'

The rain got heavier and the sky got dark. Ben was hungry and he wondered what his mum might be doing. She might be starting to cook lunch, or maybe sitting in the kitchen with a cup of tea and watching the midday movie on the little telly. She might have let Sunny inside to sit by the heater.

Ronnie flicked his smoke outside, powered the window back up and turned on the headlights. He stayed quiet the rest of the way there, but laughed to himself a few times and shook his head, like he'd thought of something funny.

After a while, the dirt road ended in some thick scrub and he stopped the car. There was another car there, a yellow van. It was old and had curtains in the back, like a caravan. Ben thought he had seen it once before, parked outside of Ronnie's, but on the opposite side of the street.

Ronnie pointed to a narrow trail leading off the gravel and twisting away through some bushes. They'd have to walk from here, he said. It was up a hill, not too far.

'I'll even let you lead the way.'

The trail was really skinny and slippery, with prickly branches that scratched your skin. It was like one Ben had been on in the Grampians when they had a school excursion last year. They'd walked to an old bluestone quarry; it had an old railway line running to it, but it was broken and rotted. Burke said that the stone from the quarry built parliament or something, but no one really cared. Fab said they should have gone to Sovereign Hill, like the grade six kids did, instead of some stupid walk to a quarry.

But this trail was quieter, apart from Ronnie's footsteps and the splatter of rain. And you couldn't see very far ahead because the shrubs were really thick and the track was winding.

Eventually, the path split and Ronnie pointed to a small clearing off to the left, where some sick-looking gum trees, grey ones, shrouded a small, rusty tin shack.

'This is it,' he said.

The shack was dark inside and smelled like the grease his dad used on the car sometimes. Ronnie stayed close behind him and shut the steel door with a heavy clank. He'd said it wouldn't take long, so Ben wondered why he shut the door behind them. He figured it was to stop the rain getting in.

There were two small windows, but they were dirty and

only a bit of light came through, so it was hard to see anything. The rain got louder, the wind stronger and the roof creaked and clattered, like some of the iron might be loose. It felt good to be out of the rain, but more than anything, Ben wanted to go home. His belly groaned. He wanted to see Sunny. And he wanted his mum.

There was a *click* and a small, yellow globe hanging above fizzled to life. 'Got a generator last month,' Ronnie said from behind him. 'Best thing I ever did.'

The roof was low and angled from the back down to the front wall. It was just one room, a rectangle of rusted corrugated iron sheets. The floor was dirty concrete and it was only four or five steps from one end to the other. Along the sides were two long timber workbenches with heavy steel vices bolted in. The back wall had one of those boards with shapes where tools were supposed to hang, but there weren't any there.

At the end of the bench near the front wall was a heavy steel stool that pivoted from the middle with a thick, greasy screw. Its green cushion was cracked and split all over. Just past the stool was a low timber bench, strung against the end wall with thick rope. It had a thin, stripy mattress rolled up on top, like one of those camping ones. A yellow pillow was at one end, but there were no sheets or blankets.

The rain was coming down harder, but he could still feel the stifled heat of the morning trapped inside those iron walls. They both stood there, quiet, as the rain drummed on the roof. Ben thought he could hear footsteps in puddles outside, but then they stopped. Ronnie hadn't moved and Ben wondered what he wanted him to do. He thought he should ask; that's what his mum would say he should do. *Like a polite young man.*

'So, what tools do you want to get?' Ben said. His voice sounded high-pitched and he hated it. He cleared his throat, concentrated, and spoke as deeply as he could. 'Which tools, I mean.'

The roof creaked and Ronnie didn't answer, but Ben could hear his breathing below the wind, deep and rough. He felt him move closer behind him.

'Be a good boy,' he said.

And the light went out.

Six

'VM: Are you feeling all right, Mr Morressi?

FM: Yeah.

VM: You look a little pale. We can pause if you like. If you need a toilet break or—

FM: Nah. Let's just get on with it.

VM: Well, you remember I mentioned earlier that we'd found something.

FM: Yes.

VM: Can you tell us anything about that?

FM: No. I mean, I don't know anything about it.

VM: I haven't told you what it is yet.

FM: Either way.

VM: Well, let me tell you something about it then. See if it jogs your memory. It was found in the Wimmera River. Does that ring a bell?

FM: No.

VM: Well, what do you think it might be?

FM: Is this some sort of riddle?

VM: You would remember if you dumped something in the river, wouldn't you?

FM: I reckon.

VM: Well, it's a rubbish bin. A local council wheelie bin.

FM: Crime of the century.

VM: Our guys at forensics think it was left there a long time ago.

FM: So?

VM: Well, forensics have told us other things about that bin.

FM: Good for them.

VM: There are human remains in that bin, Mr Morressi.

FM: Got nothing to do with me.

VM: Well, it's interesting you say that.

FM: Lots of things are interesting to you, aren't they?

VM: Forensics are pretty sure that bin belonged to you.

FM: I um... I don't know what you're talking about.

VM: Mr Morressi, we believe we can prove the bin is yours.

FM: There must be a mistake. Your forensics people. They've made a mistake.

VM: There is no mistake.

FM: I don't know...

VM: Mr Morressi, listen to me carefully. This isn't just all going to go away. Things like this don't just go away. Do you understand?

FM: I just...

VM: And we're not just going away either.

FM: I just don't know...

VM: I really think it's in your best interests to tell us what you do know.

FM: I don't think you understand... It was a long time ago...

VM: We are trying to understand, Mr Morressi. That's why we're here.

FM: But it wasn't like you think...'

Seven

They were at the beginning of a narrow trail that twisted and disappeared into the dark scrub. Fab had never been up this path before, but he knew the land well. He knew the smell of the rich volcanic earth and the sigh of wind through the trees. He knew the steep slope of the hills, the brush of the long weeds on his legs, and the sharp grass seeds scratching in his socks. It was the land of winter, of hunting, of his father.

They made their way silently up the path, with Ben leading the way.

After ten minutes or so, he stopped and pointed to a small clearing off to the left, about twenty or thirty metres from where they stood.

In the moonlight, surrounded by a clutch of thin gum trees, was a small, dark shack. It looked to be made from timber and old iron, its walls a patchwork of corrugated sheets, fibro and weatherboard – the roof low and mean. Fab thought he could see a trace of smoke from a thin chimney pipe slipping silently into the night air.

'Still wanna do it?' he said, his voice soft and low.

Ben shivered, but Fab didn't think it was from the cold.

Ben slowly shook his head. 'Maybe we should just go.'

But Fab couldn't leave things like this.

Not now.

Not now that he knew.

He squatted down and put his hands in the dirt, feeling for the biggest stone he could find.

'We going?' Ben's voice was shaky.

Fab didn't answer, but stood up, leaned back and threw the stone as hard as he could. It fizzed from his hand and disappeared until, after a brief moment of perfect stillness, he heard it crash through glass, the broken shards tinkling sweetly to the ground.

Suddenly, a yellow light lit two small windows like wolf's eyes. Fab looked across at Ben; his mouth fell open as he stared at the shack, then at Fab, then back at those yellow eyes.

Fab's heart pounded. He picked up more stones and threw them, rapid fire, toward the shack, two of them pinging on the iron roof before another one crashed through the second window.

He gripped the last stone tightly in his fingers. Then, the door creaked open ever so slightly, with a splinter of yellow light flickering through the darkness.

'Who's out there?' The voice rooted Fab to the earth. That voice. The same as in the car all those years ago.

Ben squatted low to the ground.

'Is that you, Percy? Clear off or I'll get me gun!'

Shit.

Fab dropped the stone. 'Ben,' he hissed, keeping his eyes on the shack. 'Let's go, c'mon!'

Ben was searching the ground on his hands and knees.

'Ben, forget it. C'mon, let's go!'

The door of the shack swung wide open and light spread out into the clearing. Fab could see Ronnie's figure in the doorway, tall and lean and bigger than he remembered.

'You can have the kid, Percy. See if I care! Now just fuck off!'

Then Ben stood up with a big black rock in the palm of his hand.

'Clear off, Wolfe! Ya last warning!'
Fab tried to hold him back.
'Ben, for fuck's sake!'
But Ben always had a good, strong arm.
And Ronnie never saw him coming.

Eight

The sky had become an intense blue as dusk approached and, up above the ranges, the ghost of the moon appeared. He had to hurry.

Inside the shack it was almost dark, but for the small wedges of grey light that filtered in through the broken windows. It smelled stale inside, like old furniture and engine grease. Fab felt for a light switch but there was nothing but the rough iron walls.

He stepped cautiously into the gloom, hoping his eyes would adjust. His hands met a timber bench. It was rough and grimy. He closed his eyes for a few seconds, then opened them. He could make out the walls from the nail holes of dying sunlight that broke through the iron like tiny eyes.

He moved slowly and ran his hands along the workbench. He could feel nails and screws, loose and rolling under his touch, but little else.

He put his hands under the bench and a thick spider's web entwined his fingers. He imagined a family of red-backs under there, scrambling through the weave toward the intruder. He closed his eyes, gritted his teeth and forced his hands through.

There was a timber shelf below the bench. He felt along it, the greasy dust coating his palms. His fingers knocked into a tin and it rolled and spilled a rattle of nails and screws. He pulled his hands out, wiped the black from his arms and stood up. It seemed to have gotten much darker, the eyes of light in the iron walls now dim.

He heard the clank of tin up the driveway and he flinched. Ben. At least he hoped it was Ben. But maybe someone had seen his car and... *Jesus*.

Keep it together.

He stepped further into the darkness and his head pinged on steel. He put his hands up and felt something smooth and cool – cone-shaped. Something soft brushed his ear and he swiped at it instinctively. It was a string – a cord... the light! It was a pull cord. He yanked it and there was a stiff, bakelite click. The room lit up and Fab yelped as a blackbird squawked and fluttered around the shack, before darting out a broken window.

'You all right?' Ben called from outside.

'Yep, fine.' His voice cracked. 'Just be a sec.'

The iron walls were lined with makeshift shelves made from bits of old hardwood. Jam jars half-filled with screws and mismatched washers sat like rotten teeth. Rusted tools, shrouded in dust, hung from nails ringed with baling twine.

A steel sink – an old laundry trough – was fixed against the right wall. It was filled with dirty dishes; a small tin pot sat on top with baked beans burnt inside. Between the trough and the bed was a small wood stove, its skinny chimney poking up through the roof. An axe leaned coolly against the stove – he must have used it for firewood. Fab picked it up and the weight felt good. It looked homemade, the handle fashioned from an old metal pipe, welded to the axe-head.

Jesus, could he do this? He had to help Ben, but...

A couple of old saws hung on the wall above the bed – one like a tree lopper – rusted, but thin and curved with a dark wooden handle.

He couldn't just leave things like this...

He stepped onto the bed – the mattress was soft and

thin and the frame creaked under his weight. He could feel something solid and square underfoot as he reached for the saw, like a box was squeezed under the mattress. Outside, he heard a gush of water as Ben filled a tin from the tank.

He picked up the axe and headed back toward the door. But he stopped halfway – the box under the bed. He had time to have a look. Just a quick one.

Just for a second.

It couldn't hurt.

Nine

When Fab came out of the shack he didn't say a word. He'd been in there a long time and Ben had the cement buckets ready to go, just like he'd been asked.

But Fab didn't look at the buckets. He just stood in the doorway and glared with his lips quivering like he might be upset, his fists clenched and his body stiff. He was holding a small axe, but maybe he didn't find exactly what he was looking for.

'Get out of the way,' he said.

Ben left his buckets and moved back. 'Fab, how are we gonna...'

Fab dropped the axe to the ground, then pulled a small, rusty saw from the back of his jeans. He passed it to Ben. 'Hold this,' he said, but didn't look at him when he said it.

Fab knelt and lifted Ronnic's body over onto his back. 'I've gotta get this done quick. So if you wanna look away or whatever...'

He didn't wait for an answer. He grabbed the axe, stood up, and lined it across the shinbone of Ronnie's right leg. He breathed in deeply, swung the axe high in the air above his head and brought it down with a heavy thwack.

Ben gasped as the flesh split open; it was all pink but no

blood ran out – it pooled inside the wound. He looked at Ronnie's face, like he expected him to scream out, or at least flinch a little, but he stayed frozen – his mouth stuck open.

Fab went at it like a real woodchopper. He even stripped off his shirt and was just in his white singlet, like on *Wide World of Sports*. The axe cleaved thick wounds with each swing, the meat peeling back like ripe fruit. It took a few goes before they could see the bone, shining through that pale, pink flesh. It was surprising how white it was. Fab had two big swings at the bone, but it only chipped off a couple of small pieces. It was really hard.

'Now!' Fab said, his breath a hot mist, chest heaving. He threw the axe on the ground and held his hand out. 'Give me the saw.' He took it from Ben, and ran his fingers along its serrated edge. 'It's a bit rusty,' he smiled. 'But he's not gonna mind, is he?'

Fab knelt on the ground, gripped Ronnie's ankle with his left hand and placed the saw across the hard, white bone.

'First,' he said, as he started to saw. 'First, we cut his feet off.'

Ten

It was an ill-fitting black suit that smelled like a jar of gherkins. He'd had to rely on legal aid to get him some clothes. He scratched at his neck – the collar was making him itchy. He'd even worn a tie for the first time in his life, a green one. The lawyer, for reasons she didn't explain, reckoned green was a good colour.

He looked out to the gallery – it was filling quickly with unfamiliar hard faces. City faces. Lawyers maybe. Or journalists. He wouldn't really know the difference. He scanned each row once more – maybe he might have missed her. Or maybe she was just running late.

But there was no sign, at least not yet.

At the front of the courtroom, the judge's bench rose in ornate Victorian grandeur. To the right of the bench was the dock that, while lower than the judge's bench and with fewer adornments, imposed a darker presence. There were two chairs inside. Fab's was uncomfortable, with no cushion and a hard wooden back. He hoped it wouldn't take too long, he could feel his shoulders starting to knot.

He turned toward the sudden creak of the door behind him. *Jesus Christ*... he could hardly believe it.

Ben's hair was parted carefully to one side and at first

glance he looked, in his blue suit, as though he could be part of the legal team. The suit definitely didn't come from the same place as Fab's, but it didn't look sharp and new, either, it had seen better days.

Fab tried to catch his gaze as the prison officer led Ben to his chair, but his eyes were fixed upon the gallery.

He didn't look that much different, not in the face anyway, just a bit more gaunt, his cheekbones showing through more starkly than he remembered. Fab reckoned he could have picked him in the street though, definitely. Would have known him from a mile away.

'Hey,' Fab said.

Ben just stared straight out into the court, his eyes vacant. Maybe he didn't hear him.

'Hey, Ben!'

He frowned a little, almost like he was annoyed. He started to turn and—

'No talking!' The officer grabbed Fab hard on the shoulder. 'Keep your eyes straight ahead.'

Fab took a deep breath in and out. He'd have to get a chance to talk to Ben later, surely. A chance to catch up about things. To explain.

He looked out across the courtroom – the gallery was now almost full. In front, at the bar table, was the prosecutor – a small, grey bird-like man, who somehow looked familiar. At the opposite end of the table, lost in three piles of papers, sat the defence barrister, appointed by legal aid – a fidgety woman in her late twenties with brightly dyed red hair pulled into a ponytail, serious glasses that seemed far too mature.

It looked a grave mismatch.

'All rise!' The bailiff called out gruffly and the room fell silent. In the wall behind the bench, a small redwood door opened and the judge stepped through, his wig slightly askew, a jowly red face. 'The Honourable Justice Pemmick presiding.'

Pemmick nodded to the courtroom, sat and then peered over small frameless glasses. He spoke softly. 'Please be seated.'

He looked to the bar table.

The defence barrister stood. 'Your Honour, if it pleases the court, I wish to advise that given the guilty pleas in this matter, I will be representing both defendants with respect to sentencing submissions.'

'Yes, I am aware of that Miss...' Pemmick searched his notes.

'Rosetti. *Ms* Rosetti.' She nervously pulled at the sleeve of her black gown, before sitting back in her seat.

The judge looked to the prosecution bench. 'Mr Fincke? Do you have any submissions in relation to sentencing?'

The prosecutor, in his billowing black gown, rose. 'Yes, your Honour.'

'You may proceed.'

The prosecutor studied the bar table for a moment, the room silent. Fab glanced across at Ben, who hadn't moved an inch since he sat down. He scarcely seemed to be breathing.

'Your Honour, the sentence for murder, as with all crimes, must reflect the gravity of the offence. The gravity of an offence may be weighed against many measures. For the victim, in the case of murder, it is the most grave and final act, that of the taking of one's life. For the community, the offence of murder is, appropriately, the most serious crime of our criminal statute.'

The prosecutor glanced at Fab, then back to the judge.

'But what of this crime in particular? Well, we know that it occurred almost eleven years ago, but time does not diminish its impact. At its dark core, this was a crime against a man without defences. A man who, while asleep in his home, was intruded upon by these two men — intruded upon with evil intent on that fateful November day in 1995.'

Fincke stared at Ben, then Fab.

'They went to the shack with one purpose and one purpose alone – to violently attack and kill Mr Bellamy.'

Fab looked again at Ben. He now seemed to be watching the prosecutor closely, his body arched forward and his hands linked under his chin, with thin wrists cuffed in steel.

'Mr Bellamy, a recluse and loner, had little contact with the world outside of his work. Indeed, he had moved from the township of Stawell to his shack in the Black Ranges for what one can only assume to be reasons of solitude.

'But first, let us be clear about one thing.' He paused and raised the index finger of his right hand. He slowed his speech and punched out each word that followed with a chop of his left. 'This was a crime of savage brutality.

'Your Honour, we will submit that these were cold, calculated actions. They were not carried out in the heat of the moment, or in a panic. And these actions of Mr Carver and Mr Morressi may not ever have been discovered, were it not for one critical error.'

Eleven

The river flowed close to the highway, but Fab wanted somewhere a long way into the scrub, where it was hidden, darker, and deeper. Away from the trucks, the cars and the people. A place unknown, where it could sink, rot and never be found. He urged the Sigma along the rolling dirt track and through the narrow tunnel of trees. The headlights spilled from one bend to the next and, with every bump, the bin clunked in the back seat. They had been off the highway for a while now and he knew that, eventually, the road would meet the river again.

'Wind down the window,' he said.

Above the engine he could hear it, not far away, rippling through the scrub, travelling north. He always thought it was strange how it flowed that way, like it was going uphill – against the grain and salty as the sea – sapped by farmers for generations.

But it was deep in parts; you just had to know where.

He braked and skidded the car to a stop.

Ben turned to him. 'Here?'

Fab turned off the engine. 'Here.'

* * *

Fab opened the back door and grabbed the bin by its handles. He pulled at it, but it was too heavy to manage on his own.

'Get on the other side and push.'

Ben did as he was told and gave it a shove. The bin squealed along the vinyl seat, thumped against the doorframe and fell heavily out into the gravel. Fab dropped his end on the ground, got back in the car and reversed it a little, so the headlights lit a path to the river. He left the motor running; he didn't want the battery going flat. Not out here.

Not now.

He grabbed hold of the bin again and tried to drag it through the gravel by its handles.

'I'll help.' Ben pushed from the bottom.

Fab looked at Ben and remembered the steel box back at the shack. He closed his eyes and clenched his teeth so hard, he thought they might break. They might break into small shards and tinkle sweetly, like broken glass, into his hands.

It looked like... had he really seen... was it really?

He'd have to go back. He couldn't leave it there. Where someone, anyone, one day, might find it.

He had to go back. When this was done. For Ben's sake.

* * *

The wheels slid through the gravel and Fab glanced back over his shoulder – it was only a few metres more to the water's edge and he felt a wave of relief. For the first time all day he felt like he could breathe, and the air was cool and sweet in his chest. Soon the body would be gone and—

And that's when he saw it.

'Shit!'

'What?' Ben said, crouching low at the bottom of the bin.

Fab dropped his end and put his head in his hands. 'I forgot the number.'

Ben stood up and shook his head. 'Nah, you peeled it off. Back at the shack, remember?'

'Not the street number.' Fab pointed to the side of the bin. 'There's another one. Serial number.'

74682.

He wouldn't be able to saw it out, not with the bin full of limbs and hardening cement. A wild panic rose inside him.

Leave him. Save yourself. Drive away as fast you can.

He took a long breath in and out. He steadied himself. He remembered.

'Get me the drill from the boot.'

* * *

Fab worked neatly around the numbers, each drill-hole only a few millimetres apart. Somewhere in the distance, he heard the hiss of airbrakes – a truck stopping suddenly – maybe a roo crossing the highway. They'd be back on the road soon enough and they could get away from all this. It would all be done. It was just a small setback.

After he drilled the last hole, he unfolded his pocketknife and began sawing the gaps between the drill holes. He was almost finished when a truck horn howled through the night air. He flinched, jutted the knife forward and pushed the serial number inside the bin.

'Fuck it!' He threw the knife down the road and looked up at Ben, standing like a ghost in the headlights.

'You gonna get it out?' he said.

He'd have to unscrew the bolts, open the bin and reach down inside the cement and the limbs, feel around in that cold mess of Ronnie's skin, meat and mortar.

'Nah.' He shook his head. 'What are the chances?'

Over Ben's shoulder, down the road and through the scrub, a faint yellow glow appeared behind the trees.

Headlights.

'Jesus!' Fab grabbed the handles and pulled the bin as hard as he could. He could hear it, a low rumble – an old car, or maybe a truck. He pulled with all his strength but the bin slid slowly, its wheels sinking in the gravel at the road's edge.

His feet came to the top of the embankment, from where it ran steeply down to the river. He could hear the water rushing below and see the car coming closer, the headlights now shining around the bend.

'C'mon, Ben! Help! Push it!'

Ben, who'd been watching with wide eyes, stepped in and shoved the bin with a deep groan. Fab only just got out of the way as it went rolling down the bank and crashing into the water. He looked down after it, but could see nothing other than the black ripple of the river below.

He turned back to the road, the headlights now facing them squarely from twenty metres away. The car spluttered and backfired as it pulled up beside them.

An old cream ute.

'You boys right?' Fab couldn't make out the face, but it sounded like an old farmer, his voice raspy and dry. A dog barked in a cage on the rear tray – it must sense something.

'Yeah,' Fab said. 'Car trouble. Alternator. All sorted now.'

'That right?' He slung an elbow out the window. The engine idled roughly and the dog settled into a low growl.

'Yep, all sorted,' Fab said.

He could feel the farmer's eyes, the dark face, watching, judging, knowing. He stopped breathing. He could hear the radiator fan kick and whirr, the dog jangle a chain in its cage, and Ben shift his feet slowly in the gravel.

Just leave, *leave you old bastard!*

'Righto then.'

The farmer crunched the ute into gear and slowly pulled away.

They both stood, breathless for a moment, listening and

waiting in cool disbelief until the tired whine of the engine faded into the night.

They stood there, perfectly still, until all that was left was the rush of the river and the smell of the rich, moist earth.

And their hearts, pounding blackly in their chests, pulsed with the same dark energy.

Twelve

As light filtered down the stairwell, Fab could tell from the soft white glow that the sky must be overcast. There was a chance the sun would burn through later. It was like that – the sun was sometimes hot enough to burn away the clouds.

When they went yabbying, they always had better luck if the sun was out. But sometimes they had to take the risk and head out when it was still cloudy. Sometimes, they just had to hope the sun might burn through.

As they climbed the stairs from their cells in the bowels of the court, Fab closed his eyes and listened to the hum of the street below. The car horns, tram clatter, the crush of a building site somewhere.

Unfamiliar. Alien. Exciting.

He felt a sudden desperation to be out there and to feel it. To be around people, city people, going about their day. The drab office workers in suits, the lazy-day uni students, the backpackers with clear, bright eyes and strong brown legs.

He should have moved here years ago.

It's what he would do.

When it was over.

'So, what do you reckon?'

A voice broke his daydream and Fab's eyes opened to the

sharp angles of that face and those black, sunken eyes, his arm looped by a sturdy prison officer, wrists cuffed in bright steel rings.

The first words. Since that night. Eleven years.

'Dunno,' Fab shrugged. 'It's good to see ya though.'

Ben stared at him for a moment, silent, his eyes sharpening to focus.

'A long time,' he said.

Fab nodded.

Then, as the heavy timber door back to the courtroom swung open, Ben said something else, softly, almost under his breath.

'What?' Fab said. 'I didn't hear ya.'

He said it again, but was drowned out by the growing murmur from the court.

'I didn't hear.'

Ben turned back as he was led through the door, his eyes full of tears.

'I'm sorry,' he said.

Fab shook his head. 'No, I'm the one who—'

'No more talking!' The officer, all home haircut and backyard tattoos, turned to Fab sharply. 'You know the rules.'

Fab tried to catch Ben's gaze, just to mouth the words, but he seemed to look right through him.

It was as though, in that very moment, he had finally emptied of everything.

* * *

In the courtroom, the numbers had swelled. Fab only recognised a couple of people. His mum wasn't there, but Ms Rosetti had told him she wasn't coming. Doctor's appointment or something. Fair enough. Probably better if she stayed home.

He saw Vince, the copper from the Homicide Squad. He was all right, but he never looked very happy. Maybe he had one of those faces.

His boss, that other copper, looked half-asleep. He reminded him of the coppers back in Stawell. Slow. A bit lazy.

At the front table was the prosecutor who Fab had decided looked a bit like a vampire, like Max Schreck in *Nosferatu*, but with hair. Ms Rosetti was there too and she smiled, but twitched a bit when she did it. She'd said a quick decision could go either way, but Fab saw something in her eyes that meant the opposite.

He thought he saw Ben's dad in the gallery. It looked like him, but thinner and paler looking, so he couldn't be sure of it. He looked out for Lucy, but still no sign.

Near the front, someone put their hand up and waved with fingers spread wide apart – like they were miming a window washer. Fab sat up in his chair and saw the sheepish smile and those round brown cheeks.

Afriki.

Fab smiled, but Ms Rosetti caught his eye, frowned, and shook her head. Fab wondered if Afriki had moved yet, or if he'd taken a couple of days off to—

Then that little timber door behind the judge's bench creaked open.

'All rise. The Honourable Justice Pemmick presiding.'

The judge raised his eyes briefly to the courtroom. 'Be seated,' he said.

'Mr Benjamin Carver,' the judge turned to Ben. Jesus, it was gonna happen now. So fast. Fab could feel the floor begin to vibrate. It was Ben, bouncing his leg.

'Mr Carver, you have pleaded guilty to the murder of Mr Ronald Bellamy and there are certain matters I must consider when formulating the sentence for your crime.

'The crime of murder is the most serious in our criminal jurisdiction and carries with it the most severe maximum penalty, that of imprisonment for life. The imposition of such a penalty is an extremely grave matter and not one which is ever taken without deep consideration.'

Fab felt his throat constrict as the judge launched into a summary of the evidence. Then, he got to the guts of it.

'I accept the submission of the defence that the crime itself was unplanned, without premeditation and largely spontaneous. Indeed, were it not for the spectre of child sexual abuse, it would be almost inexplicable.

'Furthermore, I do accept the submissions that it is indeed possible, if not likely, that Mr Bellamy and others committed grossly indecent acts against you. The relevance of the information you have provided to police – and the corroboration of Mr Morressi, to the extent he is able – suggest that it was not a concoction.

'Moreover, Mr Bellamy's prior offending heightens the prospect that you are telling the truth. Indeed,' he looked to the prosecutor, 'the court has not been presented with a credible alternative motive. As such, I am prepared to accept you were driven solely by revenge. It appears it was a crime committed without planning or forethought.'

Ben stopped bouncing his leg.

'Away from Mr Bellamy, you were able to build the foundations of a positive future. You were, to appearances at least, able to overcome the pain of your past.

'Undoubtedly, what occurred on that November day was a terrible act that you would live to regret. But I am willing to accept the submissions that you were deeply damaged by the violations perpetrated against you by Bellamy and, it would appear, others who formed part of a vile paedophile ring where children were groomed and shared.

'I trust that the police will be pursuing certain matters arising from and relevant to this case with some haste, and that your continued cooperation will be instrumental in those investigations. I am limited, however, in the extent to which such cooperation may be brought to bear when considering your sentence, given those matters are yet to be concluded.

'Nonetheless, in formulating your sentence, I do have

regard for the abuse as a mitigating factor, despite your clear culpability for the offence of murder.'

The judge took off his glasses and looked at Ben directly.

'Ideally, Mr Carver, as suggested by the prosecution, you should have reported your allegations against Mr Bellamy at the time, so that the police may have investigated it. But I accept that this may have been something you did not want to expose. Indeed, the impact of such events would be compounded in a country town, where it is difficult to maintain privacy over one's affairs.

'It is nevertheless important that the community understands that people cannot take the law into their own hands. Your actions in savagely beating Mr Bellamy to death were grossly violent. The cooler heads in our community, quite rightly, have an expectation that individuals are not subject to violent retribution, however aggrieved one may be.

'On the other hand, the community holds the violation of children, especially sexually, as among the most vile and despised acts. Children should be protected from the depravity of people such as Mr Bellamy, and those like him. And it is understandable that a deep well of anger exists within the victims of such acts. Thus, many may well regard your crime, while extremely serious, as less grave than acts of murder motivated by jealousy, greed or malice.

'However, I must have regard for general deterrence, as is required by the Act. It is this aspect that I have grappled with most extensively. While I have sympathy for your individual situation, the weight of the law must have regard for more utilitarian purposes – that is to say, the greater good of the community. In this respect, I am concerned that anything less than a severe sentence may be viewed as a lessening of culpability for crimes such as yours. It is against this test that I must weigh your individual circumstances.'

Ms Rosetti looked very pale, almost like she hadn't breathed.

'Finally, with respect to the disposal of the body, I accept the submissions from your counsel and the prosecution that you were neither the architect of, nor the primary actor in the dismemberment and disposal of the corpse of Mr Bellamy. Indeed, on the evidence presented, I accept that it is likely you were in a state of shock in the aftermath of your crime.' The judge took off his glasses. 'Mr Carver, please rise.'

Very slowly, Ben stood. He straightened his jacket a little, and then looked up with his chin jutting out.

'Mr Benjamin Matthew Carver, for the murder of Mr Ronald Bellamy, you are sentenced to a term of seven years imprisonment, with a non-parole period of four years.'

There was a murmur around the court, but Ben didn't make a sound.

Seven? Four? Didn't sound too bad. Not bad at all.

Ben put his hands on the edge of the dock, his fingers trembling.

'Silence, please,' the judge said. A hush returned to the room. 'Mr Carver, you may sit.'

As Ben sat back down, Fab looked at the judge squarely and felt a burn in his belly. The room suddenly swam, the walls heaving up and down, the faces all a blur.

Jesus Christ.

He closed his eyes, breathed deeply, and tried to calm himself. He opened his eyes and looked at Ms Rosetti, who smiled and nodded at him like it was going well. He swallowed drily and turned back to the judge.

'Mr Fabrizio Morressi, you have pleaded guilty to being an accessory after the fact to the murder of Ronald Bellamy.'

Morr-*essi*, not Morrissey. Not even the judge could get it right. Out in the gallery, Afriki smiled and gave him a thumbs up. That was new.

'And his life was ended in a savage manner...'

Fab had a thought intrude, a pleasant one. Lucy. He closed his eyes again and pictured her. She would have wanted to come, but Bob wouldn't have let her. He would have said they couldn't close the kitchen, or that his back was playing up, or some other bullshit. Either way, it didn't really matter now.

'...he was evidently a dark presence in your friend's life and this coloured your judgement...'

He thought about her soft doe eyes and the way she smelled like strawberry in the afternoon, then schnitzel at night. And he wondered, as he had done almost every hour of every day since, whether she had come to his house. He wondered if she'd come to tell him she would leave Bob after all. Maybe she was there that afternoon, with her bags, knocking on his door, but he was already gone. The more he thought about it, the more he was convinced it was true.

'...I have also considered your character. You were apparently gainfully employed, but with few associations outside of your workplace...'

Where would they put him? Ms Rosetti reckoned if it was a decent term, he might get medium security. Maybe Beechworth, not Port Phillip or Barwon.

Where was Pokey? Was it Barwon?

If he ended up there, there'd be trouble for sure. But if it was a light sentence, maybe it'd be a prison farm, Dhurringile or somewhere, minimum security. That would be even better. Lucy might be able to visit, if she had time. They could keep in touch. Either way, he would write to her. Call her if he could, but only if it didn't cause her too much trouble with Bob. Then, once he got out, they could start over.

'...Mr Morressi...'

What would the beds be like? A stretcher type or a mattress? Hopefully a mattress. Nothing fancy. Just as long as it was firm.

'Mr Morressi...'

There'd be a telly either way, so it wouldn't be too bad. Could even keep fit too, out in the yard. Lucy would be impressed if he kept himself in shape – and there'd be no booze or dope to lead him astray. Hopefully Ben would be at the same place. If not, he'd try to get transferred to where he was. It was like a second chance in some ways. They could keep an eye out for each—

'*Mr Morressi!*'

He opened his eyes and turned to the judge. His face was crimson.

'I am giving the reasons for your sentence, so I suggest it is not the time to daydream!'

'Sorry, your Honour.'

The judge nodded and returned to his notes. 'Mr Morressi. I accept the submission of your counsel, insofar as your actions were motivated principally in protection of your friend, the codefendant in this trial. It is possible that, if one is to accept that sexual abuse has occurred, you may have felt some degree of guilt that you hadn't done all in your power to stop it occurring.'

Fab glanced at Ben and felt his guts sink.

'But I suggest to you that such remorse is misplaced. As a child, even if you had been certain of the abuse, there was, most likely, little you could have done to prevent it. But these feelings of guilt do not, in my assessment, amount to a significant mitigation of your culpability.'

Pemmick leaned forward.

'These are very serious matters. You went to great lengths to conceal the crime. And your actions constitute the most serious violation of a corpse I have come across in twenty-three years on the bench. According to the forensic evidence, you savagely dismembered the corpse of Mr Bellamy in the most grotesque fashion. It would seem to indicate that you may have derived some perverse pleasure from the act. Moreover, you came prepared with the bin, demonstrating a high degree of forethought.

'Mr Morressi, you mutilated the corpse of Mr Bellamy in the most horrific way imaginable. This is a serious aggravating factor in my consideration of your sentence. Your disposal of his remains in a rubbish bin heightens the inhumanity of your actions. And you were just eighteen years old! I have much difficulty understanding how a young man could so easily be given to such peculiar acts of gross violence.

'The maximum sentence for the crime of being accessory after the fact to murder is the same as that of murder, life imprisonment. In sentencing, I must have regard for the nature and gravity of the offence, which is, in this case, amongst the most serious I have encountered.

'The suggestion of the sexual abuse of Mr Carver, while a mitigating factor in his defence, is not sufficient to warrant a diminution of your sentence.

'The fact that you left the scene, planned and thought through your actions, shows a level of calculation. Had you acted purely on the spur of the moment, then that would have been a different matter. But you had time to consider and weigh up your decisions. You would now know, certainly, that you chose very poorly. 'Mr Morressi, you committed acts of utter savagery. While you were witness to the murder and this should have affected you, you seemed unencumbered by emotion or fear. You had a clear choice. You could have gone to the police and reported what occurred, while still offering support to your friend. Indeed, if sentenced as a juvenile, Mr Carver would have been a free man today.

'It is important that the community are reminded that assisting another person to conceal a serious crime, whatever the motivation, carries a significant penalty. I can accept that a decision to turn in your friend to the police would have required great courage. But it is vital to the maintenance of a civil society that those who attempt to conceal such crimes are punished. And it remains, despite the circumstances of your friend, difficult to fully understand your motivation.'

But you don't know the things I saw.

'I accept the submissions of your counsel, insofar as your initial actions were to protect your friend in an act of loyalty, however misguided. But your subsequent actions in returning to the scene and the callousness with which the corpse was handled, indicate a frightening level of detachment, bordering on psychotic.'

No one knows the things I saw.

'The brutality with which you handled the body is a disturbing insight into your capabilities. I am concerned that you are indeed capable, if not likely, to commit serious crimes in the future. And, for this reason above all others, you must be separated from the community. Mr Morressi, please rise.'

I hid it down the mineshaft.

'Mr Fabrizio Morressi, for being an accessory after the fact to the murder of Mr Ronald Bellamy, you are sentenced to a maximum of nine years imprisonment, with a non-parole period of six years.'

And it goes almost to the centre of the earth.

Thirteen

Every night, after the customers had left and Bob had gone to bed, Lucy mixed herself a special Southern and Coke with a double shot. Instead of the cheap, syrupy cola from the dispenser, she'd open a can of Coke from the fridge, pour in just enough, then tip the rest down the sink.

She would sit and smoke in the bar on her own, with the lights off and the blinds pulled down, and the television casting a dim blue haze. Her eyes would be on the telly, but she was never really watching.

And she'd quietly drift away from the pub, the town and its people.

* * *

When they were sentenced, it was the afternoon and the regulars were all in. She heard it on the radio. It was on the news. They all heard it.

Lucy didn't say a word, but quietly mixed her special drink, left Bob in the bar, and walked to the kitchen. She went through the swinging doors, past the broken dishwasher Bob bought from the *Trading Post*, and into the cool darkness of the pantry. She didn't turn on the light, but closed the door behind her, and sat down on a barrel of cooking fat.

She sat there with the cans of tomatoes, buckets of mayonnaise and tins of beetroot slices. She sat there, alone in that dark and quiet place.

And, with her special drink untouched, her chest heaved deep and raw.

* * *

Two months later, on a Wednesday afternoon, Lucy stood in the empty bar as the stark afternoon light shone through the windows. She looked out to the supermarket across the road, where three crows picked through someone's unwanted lunch. Nearby, two African boys were doing the trolleys, both quiet and careful in their movements as they linked them in two long trains.

The locals would all still be chattering, but not for much longer. People would stop talking soon and start to forget. Some things, they would figure, were best forgotten.

At around five o'clock the cars would start to pull up with the regulars. Bernie and the rest of them – the barely functioning alcoholics who came for five or six pots and a bowl of chips, before driving home to their lucky wives.

They ogled her, she knew that. She'd see them in the mirror, sneaking looks at her legs, her arse, the eyes quickly scanning up and down before she turned. Then, after a couple of beers they'd get bolder, openly staring at her breasts as she served pot after pot, the smile hurting her cheeks.

She let it go. She had to. But the thought of them and their eyes still made her feel sick.

* * *

Bob was asleep upstairs. If he woke, she'd say she had a migraine, but he'd likely be out on his lilo for a while yet. She lit a cigarette, walked to the front of the bar, closed the latch and pulled the blinds down low.

'Hello?'

A voice outside. She stopped for a moment, hesitated. She moved in close to the blind, the dry, dusty weave rough against her cheek.

'Hello?'

It was unfamiliar. A man's voice. Youngish, but not local. Definitely not local. He knocked on the glass.

'Anyone there? You open?'

She stole a look around the blind, the light stinging her eyes. A suit and dark hair. She drew back into the shadows and pulled hard on her cigarette.

Jesus.

It was that copper. What the hell did he want?

She took another drag. Something about Fab? Something happen in jail? She stubbed out the cigarette and cleared her throat.

'Sorry, won't be a second!' she said, in her best voice.

The blind whizzed up and he stared at her through the glass with a smirk, as though he knew she was there all along. Lucy pulled down the latch and pushed the door open.

'Thought you must have closed up,' he said. 'Saw the blind come down.'

'Oh no,' she said, a smile in her voice. 'It's just that this light here is so bright. Bob, my husband, he reckons it's bad for the pool table.'

She held the door open and he walked slowly inside. She watched his face for any sign of news. Nothing. He looked different than she remembered. Older, his eyes ringed with deep shadows.

He stopped a few steps in and surveyed the room. 'Quiet today?'

'Quiet every day,' Lucy trotted briskly for the safety of the bar. She never liked being out on the floor. Too exposed. 'Regulars start in about five, so if you're looking for company they—'

'Just a drink really.' He walked up to the bar, sat on a stool and turned toward her. 'A pot of Carlton will do. Name's Vince.'

Lucy headed for the glass chiller, a stainless steel chamber Bob bought years ago, and got a pot from the cold end. It was icy and the glass stuck to her fingers.

'We've met before,' she said.

He cleared his throat. 'Really?'

'I'm sure of it.'

He nodded. 'You might be right.'

She went back to the taps, but remembered the Carlton hadn't been poured since lunchtime. She turned and caught Vince staring at his feet, lost in thought.

'Is a stubby okay instead?' she said.

He looked up. 'That's fine. Tap trouble?'

'It just saves me pouring out a whole jug of foam for nothing.' She shrugged. 'Well, not for nothing... I just mean —'

'It's okay.' Vince smiled. 'I used to do bar work myself. The lines get warm when they haven't been poured in a while.'

Lucy placed the glass and the stubby in front of him. She leaned back against the chiller and crossed her arms. He looked at her with raised eyebrows and she suddenly realised she'd left the top on the beer.

'Sorry, one of the regulars likes it unopened.' She cracked off the lid. 'Force of habit.'

'Really?' Vince said, taking the stubby in his hand. 'Why's he like it like that?'

Lucy stiffened and stared at Vince. She felt her face tighten. 'I never thought to ask him.' She looked down at the bar where the laminate was worn almost right through from the elbows and the glasses and the years.

The bug zapper fizzled a victim as their eyes met and held for the first time.

'I've been to see him,' he said.

She bit her bottom lip.

'How is he?'

'Coping. I went to tell him...'

'Ben?'

'Yes.'

'How did he—'

'Not well. The coroner will investigate, but it looks straight-forward. It seems he tore up a sheet and—'

'I read about it.'

She stared at Vince.

He took a swig of his beer.

'It's not right what happened,' she said.

'With Ben?'

'No, I...'

'The sentences? Well, we didn't expect—'

'No, none of it. From the start.' She looked down at the floor. 'From when they were boys.'

Vince put the stubby back on the bar and nodded.

Lucy felt the heat rush to her cheeks. She leaned back and gripped the cold steel edge of the chiller behind her. She shook her head.

'You don't know what it's like here with—'

She stopped herself and stared out the window to the supermarket, out to where she'd watch him push the trolleys around, smiling with that African boy.

She took a deep breath in and out. 'Why did you come?'

The zapper electrified another blowie. Vince reached into his jacket pocket.

'Had to give you something.'

He opened his hand to reveal an old grey rabbit's foot, crudely pierced with a ring of steel. He shrugged. 'He wants you to have it.'

Lucy picked it up from his hand and studied it closely. 'Why?'

'He didn't say.'

'No, I mean, why did you come? Why all this way, just for this?'

'I've got some other business here.'

'Like what?'

'Well, once he found out Ben was gone, there was certain information Fab was able to provide.'

'What kind of—'

'I can't answer that.'

She rolled the rabbit's foot across her fingers, feeling the thin bone within.

'You know, I used to see him looking at this sometimes, while he was in the bar.'

Vince took a sip of his beer.

'Sometimes when he was over the road too. He'd get this distant look in his eyes.' She pushed it into her apron pocket. 'When he was a bit drunk one night, he told me his father gave it to him. Only time he ever mentioned him.'

'I think it's meant to be good luck.'

'Luck?' Lucy picked up her smokes from beside the till and slid a smooth white filter from the packet. 'Lot of good it did him.' She leaned back against the till, lit up, and glared at Vince through the smoke. 'And a lot of good it did that rabbit.'

She glanced at his half-full stubby, then looked hard into his eyes. 'Did you want another beer, or...'

'Don't worry, I get the message. I'll make this one a traveller.'

He picked up his stubby, dropped a five-dollar note on the bar and turned for the door. 'Thanks for the beer.'

As he walked away, Lucy reached into her apron and gripped the rabbit's foot tight in her fingers; her heart squeezed and gave out one heavy thump.

'Listen,' she said. He turned back.

'Thanks for coming.'

He smiled thinly. 'No worries.'

She butted out her cigarette. 'If you see him, tell him thanks.'

He nodded. 'I will.'

'And tell him I'll come. Soon.'

'Yep.' He pushed open the door.

'And tell him I...'

He looked back, the door half open.

'Tell him I... that I changed my mind.'

'About?'

'He'll know.'

Vince nodded. 'Yeah, I will then. If I see him.'

And she watched him walk slowly into that bright white light.

Acknowledgements

M y heartfelt thanks to all who have helped.
I am especially grateful to Vanessa Radnidge for her passion and belief. Deepest thanks also to Grace Heifetz for her brilliant insights and steadfast support (and for spotting *Wimmera* in the slush pile).

My sincere thanks to all the outstanding team at Hachette Australia, especially Fiona Hazard, Louise Sherwin-Stark, Justin Ractliffe, Daniel Pilkington, Thomas Saras, Jordan Weaver-Keeney, and Tom Bailey-Smith.

I am also grateful to Deonie Fiford for her forensic eye, and to Christa Moffitt for the most perfect cover imaginable.

The threads of this novel were first woven in the RMIT Professional Writing program (special thanks to Ania Walwicz); along its journey, it received precious support from Varuna – The Writers House, Writers Victoria (especially Kate Larsen), and the NSW Writers Centre.

To the literary prizes who saw some glimmer in this dark tale – especially the British Crime Writers' Association Dagger Awards, the Victorian Premier's Literary Awards, and the Impress Prize – your recognition was invaluable.

Thank you to those who read my early drafts: Tania

Chandler, Melissa Manning, Jennifer Porter, Susi Fox, and Meg Dunley.

To my family, thanks for (almost) understanding why I quit my career – especially my mum and dad, who will always inspire me. To my brothers – Jim, Roy, and Gary – thank you for introducing me to the world of books.

To Andy McCann, my grade six teacher (and best teacher I ever had) – thank you.

Lastly, I am indebted to Georgia for her unfailing love and belief. And to Bridie, who was there.

COME VISIT US AT
WWW.LEGENDPRESS.CO.UK

FOLLOW US
@LEGEND_PRESS